# MY COUSIN IS A TIME TRAVELLER

## DAVID SOLOMONS

nosy
crow

First published in the UK in 2019 by Nosy Crow Ltd
The Crow's Nest, 14 Baden Place
Crosby Row, London, SE1 1YW, UK

www.nosycrow.com

ISBN: 978 0 85763 992 9

Nosy Crow and associated logos are trademarks and/or registered
trademarks of Nosy Crow Ltd

Text copyright © David Solomons, 2019
Cover and inside illustrations copyright © Robin Boyden, 2019

The right of David Solomons to be identified as the author of this work has
been asserted.

A CIP catalogue record for this book is available from the
British Library.

Printed and bound in Great Britain by Clays Ltd, Elcograf S.p.A
Typeset by Tiger Media

Papers used by Nosy Crow are made from wood grown in sustainable forests

3 5 7 9 10 8 6 4 2

*For Luke and Lara*

*and their cousins Daniel and Ridley.*

# 1
# THAT'S THE WAY THE WOOKIE CRUMBLES

I leaned on my bedroom windowsill and gazed out at the searchlight's vivid beam reaching up from the roof of the Civic Centre, illuminating the underside of the clouds with the letters "SL". They stood for Star Lad. To the wider world he was a superhero, but I knew him as Zack Parker, my big brother. So far, during his short career, he'd saved Earth from, in order: a giant asteroid and a comic-book-store-owning supervillain; alien invaders disguised as my gym teacher; a world-eating Top Trump card; my Evil Twin; and a particularly annoying brain-in-a-jar and her sister. Those were his big, end-of-the-world missions, but in his role as

Earth's saviour he also carried out a host of lesser duties in between. He was out there now, no doubt rescuing some small child from a rampaging robot, or catching a falling plane, or rounding up some criminal kingpin and his henchmen.

There was a distant rumble and the horizon burst into light, the explosion sending bright-orange flames into the sky to silhouette the rooftops of our home town of Bromley.

Had to be Zack.

I might learn the details of tonight's adventure when he returned later, but in all likelihood the only thing I'd get from him would be a grunt as he pushed past me to the fridge for a snack. He was always hungry after a mission. That was his style: peckish after, and reluctant before. He'd never wanted the responsibility of being a superhero, not from that first moment when a purple-caped, egg-headed alien called Zorbon the Decider had chosen him to save the world. Zack couldn't see the point of having powers and it was never far from his thoughts. Earlier that evening he'd brought it up for the gazillionth time.

"And another thing," he'd said as we washed up the dinner dishes together. "Superheroes are expensive."

"But you don't get paid," I reminded him. "You're a

free service. Like that antivirus software Dad uses."

"Yes, but there are costs associated with my exploits. Have you read the council's latest annual report?"

"Is this a trick question?"

He scrubbed vigorously at the bottom of a pot. "It's all in there. Itemised. The clean-up bill from just one interdimensional monster attack means they've had to find savings elsewhere in the budget. Did you know we're down to a fortnightly bin collection?"

I did not. And I didn't care.

"That's not all." He was getting into his stride. "I am just one hero, which means I can only deal with one incident at a time."

"But you're not alone. You've got Dark Flutter." That was the superhero identity of our neighbour Lara Lee. She too had been turned into a superhero by Zorbon, but her powers were rather more limited than Zack's. Essentially, she could talk to fluffy animals.

"Fine, so there are two of us. Great." He shrugged. "So let's take firefighting, just as an example. Think how many more fires twenty new firemen could deal with compared with just two superheroes. See, we're expensive and inefficient."

Studying the blaze on the horizon I caught a whiff of burning in the night air and I thought about what

Zack had said. Were superheroes a waste of money? But without Star Lad, Earth would've been flattened by a giant asteroid, invaded by aliens, swallowed whole, or ripped apart by quantum forces. That stuff was more important than a weekly bin collection. And anyway, I liked living in a world with superheroes.

I yawned. My best friend, Serge, says that I sound like an exhausted Wookie when I yawn. It had been a long day; I'd expended a great deal of effort in avoiding a significant amount of maths and English homework. Before I went to bed I made sure to leave the window wide open for Zack to fly through when he did eventually come home. In that regard he was a bit like Peter Pan, but without the green tights and the curious attachment to fairies. Like the rest of the world, I felt safe with him out there. But unlike them, I realised as I rested my head on my Spider-Man pillow, I felt safe with him in here too. And as I drifted off into a superhero dream-filled sleep it struck me, not for the first time, that I liked living in a world with Zack. Not that I'd ever admit it to his face.

"Wake up."

I was flying in my dreams when Zack's voice brought me down to earth like a well-aimed kryptonite-tipped arrow. I sat up in bed, startled by the urgency of his tone. My eyes slowly adjusted to the fuzzy dark. The streetlight outside my still-open window splashed an orange glow across the bedroom floor where I saw Zack pacing anxiously. He was wearing his Star Lad costume and his cape flicked out as he turned. His mask was pushed off his face and rested against his forehead. I glanced at my Green Lantern alarm clock on the bedside table. Three a.m.

"Must have been some night," I said. "You want to tell me about it?"

He peeled off the cape and folded it neatly into a square, tucking it under one arm. "False alarm. They didn't need me."

"But what about the explosion and the fire?"

"Someone was burning rubbish in their garden and it got out of control." He removed his mask. "The fire brigade dealt with it."

I propped myself up on my elbows. "So what have you been doing all this time?"

"Thinking," he said. I didn't like the way he said it. "I sent a message to Zorbon using my telepathic power. I've asked him to come over tomorrow."

That was weird. Usually Zorbon showed up unannounced with a dire prophecy about the end of the

5

world, which inevitably led to a mission for Star Lad and the rest of us. To my knowledge this was the first time that Zack had called him. I felt a creeping sense of unease.

"Luke, I've made a decision." Zack paused, and by the light of the streetlamp I could see his face knot up with concern. "I'm getting rid of my superpowers."

# 2
# AVENGERS ASSEMBLY

"Are they transferable?"

That was the first question Serge asked me at school the next morning when I told him about Zack's terrible decision.

I shook my head sadly. It had been my question too when Zack informed me of his intention. If my brother didn't want his powers, then I was happy to take them on. But when I'd said that last night he had shown only irritation, and then he'd stormed out of my bedroom. Though not before pausing in the doorway to drop another bombshell.

"Things are about to change," he'd said.

"Well, *duh*," I'd snapped.

"I'm not just talking about the superpowers," he'd said. "Other stuff too. Big stuff."

What could possibly be bigger than giving up being Star Lad?

"Listen to me," Zack had said. "As much as you want it to, the world can't stay the same forever."

He was speaking in riddles. "Is this about another invasion? Is Earth about to fall off its axis? What did Zorbon tell you?"

For a moment I'd thought he was about to say more, but he stopped himself. His expression softened and he fixed me with a kindly smile.

"G'night, Luke."

The door clicked as he closed it behind him.

I was no clearer about his puzzling words the following day, as Serge and I filed into the gym alongside the rest of our year group for a special assembly. We sat cross-legged on the floor while teachers patrolled the lines, watching beadily and calling for silence whenever it was broken.

"Is Zack certain that Zorbon *can* remove his powers?" Serge pondered.

"He bestowed them in the first place," I said. In comics, superpowers were always "bestowed" not simply "given".

"*Oui*, but it is not like receiving a gift of, for example…" Serge hummed as he contemplated the most fitting comparison. "A pineapple. You cannot simply say: please now remove my pineapple."

Serge was right – Zack's powers weren't like a pineapple. They were as much a part of him now as his love for algebra and dislike of comics. Leaving aside the finer points of superpower removal, there was still time before Zorbon arrived at the weekend for me to do something. Between now and then I had to persuade Zack to change his mind.

"I'm calling an emergency S.C.A.R.F. meeting," I whispered. S.C.A.R.F. was the Superhero Covert Alliance Reaction Force, an organisation set up by Serge and me to work alongside Star Lad and Dark Flutter. This might very well be its most important mission yet. "Today, after school, in the tree house. Zack will listen to all of us if we put on a united front."

Serge glanced along the line of seated classmates. I followed his gaze to a girl with short dark hair and a lightly freckled face. Her hands were folded neatly in her lap and her bright, intelligent eyes peered straight ahead at the stage. She was Lara Lee – friend, neighbour and Dark Flutter.

"I am not sure how united we will be," Serge said quietly.

I understood what he meant. During our latest adventure, on a fateful minibreak to Great Minds Leisure Park, we had encountered an evil brain-in-a-jar with incredible mind powers. There had been a lot of body-swap shenanigans, in the course of which Serge and Lara had briefly occupied one another's bodies. That wouldn't have been so bad, but they were boyfriend and girlfriend at the time. Their relationship hadn't survived the switcheroo, and now things between them were awkward, to say the least.

"C'mon, Serge, pull yourself together. This is more important than all that lovey-dovey stuff, this is about something deep and meaningful." I laid a hand on his shoulder and fixed him in the eye. *"Superheroes."*

He offered me a faltering smile and then looked down at the floor with a sigh.

Our headteacher, Mr Hines, took to the stage and clapped for our attention. Lingering conversations dwindled into silence. Standing beside Mr Hines was a man I didn't recognise. He had thick dark hair with a white streak down the middle of his head, as if he was wearing a badger. He was dressed in a stripy shirt and jeans and slung over one shoulder was a canvas bag with the words "Books Are My Bag" on the front. Even from where I was sitting near the back of the hall I could tell that he was sweating.

"Who's this guy?" I asked Serge.

"You do not know?" He sounded surprised. "The posters have been up all over school for some time. Did you not receive the letter to take home to your parents? And the two subsequent reminder letters?"

Now that he mentioned it I vaguely remembered tucking a series of correspondence from the school office in my bag. I was fairly confident the letters were still in there, possibly next to a month-old banana.

"He is Arthur Veezat," said Serge, lowering his voice so as not to attract the attention of a nearby teacher.

"Is he French then?"

"Hmm?" Serge gave me a strange look. "*Non*, I said that he is our *author visit*."

Now I understood. The school occasionally drafted in children's authors in an effort to inspire us with their stirring personal stories of how they came to write a book none of us had ever heard of. Mr Hines introduced him and I listened for about five minutes as the author jumped about the stage, gesticulating wildly and shouting out words like "plot", "character" and "royalties". But I was too busy thinking about Zack and our important S.C.A.R.F. business to take in much of what he was saying. After a while he calmed down and read a chapter from his book. I felt myself lulled to sleep as his monotonous voice drifted over the hall.

When the reading was finally over Serge turned to me and said, "Our adventures are far more interesting than his. Per'aps we should write them down also."

He was forgetting one thing. "But then everyone who reads them would discover Star Lad and Dark Flutter's true identities." I still cared about that stuff, even if Zack was ready to throw it all away.

"We could change the names. Instead of Luke and Serge, we will be Lionel and Steve. And instead of Star Lad and Dark Flutter…" He frowned in silence. Superhero names were tricky, all the good ones having been taken. "I will get back to you on that."

In fact, recording our adventures was something that had occurred to me some time ago. A lot had happened since Zorbon's first visit to the tree house and I would hate to forget a single detail, so I had been writing down our missions in a series of superhero-themed notebooks that Serge had given me for my last birthday. I'd already covered our first adventure with the Nemesis asteroid, the invasion by alien gym teachers, Gordon the World-Eater, and my trip to a parallel Earth to confront my Evil

Twin. One day I would be as ancient and forgetful as my dad, so it would be nice to have a record.

The author didn't exactly finish his presentation with a bang. It sort of just fizzled out and then the teachers realised it was over and we clapped a bit and the assembly came to an end. As the classes filed out in their usual disorderly fashion, the author took a seat at a table piled high with his books. He uncapped a pen and watched the departing children with an expression of sad resignation. The hall emptied until there was just me and a handful of others, including Serge and Lara. We trickled over to his table, forming a short queue, and a minute and a half later I was at the front, face-to-face with Arthur Veezat, or whatever his name was.

His features creased into a question. "Have we met before?"

"I don't think so."

"You look familiar. Maybe when I visited your school last year?"

I shook my head. "You're the first author I've ever met."

"That's not true," Lara interjected. "You've met my aunt Farah."

"I thought she was a dentist."

"She's an author-dontist. She says there's no money

in books, so she fixes people's teeth for cash and writes stories for fun."

I could see a confused expression appear on Arthur's face. Lara had that effect on people. But there was no point arguing with her. He plucked one of his books from the top of a pile, opened it and hovered his pen above the page.

"So what's your name, young man?" he enquired.

"Luke," I said.

He beamed up at me. "That's my son's name too." He began to write it in the book. "To Luke," he said as he scribbled.

Standing in front of a real author, even one as lame as Arthur, got me thinking about my own writing. Maybe Arthur could offer me some tips.

"I'm writing a book," I said. "Any advice?"

"You mean apart from all that insightful writing advice I imparted during my fun-filled presentation?"

"Exactly." I leaned in. "I want the good stuff. The under-the-counter advice. The *secret* to writing."

"I don't think there's a secret, but one thing I would say – know how it ends." He gestured to the stack of books. "This is the last in my series. I knew how it would end way back when I began the first one." He paused. "I wrote them for my children. For my Luke, and my little girl, Lara."

"That's my name," said Lara delightedly, and then she caught Serge's eye and they scowled at each other.

"My kids are grown up now," Arthur said with a deep sigh, "so it's time to bring these stories to a conclusion." He laid a hand on the cover and a glazed expression came over his face. Not glazed like a doughnut – the other kind where you stare unfixed into the distance. Either he'd forgotten what he was about to say again, or he was lost in thought.

Serge cleared his throat. "Do you *per'aps* have a third child whose name is Serge?"

Arthur laughed. "Sorry, Serge." He slid the book he'd been writing in across the table to me. "Six ninety-nine."

"Excuse me?"

"For the book." He tapped the price, which was clearly labelled on the back cover.

"Why would I want a book?"

He looked baffled. "You're in the signing queue."

Serge stepped in front of me, unzipping a small leather wallet and producing a wad of notes from inside. "Please forgive my friend. I should like to purchase your complete *oeuvre*." He handed over the cash and we waited while Arthur happily signed each of the five books in the series.

"Here," Arthur said, pushing the same book into my hands. "It's already signed to you – you might as well have it."

I hesitated, staring suspiciously at it. "Does the main character's dad have a silver filigree pocket-watch that's been handed down through the generations?"

Arthur looked puzzled. "Is that important?"

I nodded. "It's a sure sign that the dad's going to die. And I can't be doing with any of that."

"Just take the book, Luke," he said through gritted teeth.

After that, Lara bought the latest one, saying they were her favourites, which I knew was a lie because I'd seen her bookshelves and they're full of miserable novels about growing up, which, to give him credit, Arthur's were not. We thanked him and headed out. I could feel his eyes on us as we crossed the gym, and when we reached the door he called out.

"Goodbye, Luke, Lara and Serge. It was lovely meeting you all. And remember, we are all the heroes of our own stories."

He smiled at us and we waved back.

"He's a bit strange," I muttered to the others. "Probably all that time spent alone in a room talking to imaginary people."

We left the gym and made our way along the corridor to our next class. Know the ending, Arthur had advised. Useless. I was writing down real life, so there was no way of knowing. But at that moment, not in my wildest imagination, could I have pictured how my own story would end.

# 3
# THE DEPUTY MANAGER
# WHO FELL TO EARTH

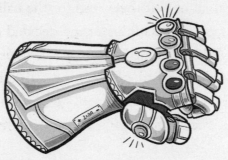

It was later that same day and I was at Dad's comic shop on the High Street, waiting for him to close up so we could go home together. I wanted to get to the tree house to prepare for the S.C.A.R.F. meeting that evening, but in the meantime I had settled myself behind the till with a Thor-themed pad and a pencil with a Mjolnir hammer rubber on the end, in order to write down more of our recent adventures. I'd already written tons, filling eight pages of narrow-lined A4. Both sides. As I put the finishing touches to the latest section I wondered what our next adventure would be, and then I got this sick feeling in my stomach as it hit me – there might not be another one if Zack gave up his superpowers. Without Star Lad, there could be no S.C.A.R.F. (As much as Dark Flutter was a superhero, Star Lad was the heart of the team.) Couldn't Zack see how selfish he was being? I didn't want our adventures to end. Once again I bitterly reflected that I would have made a much more committed superhero than my brother. And for the trillionth time I asked myself why hadn't Zorbon decided on me, not Zack? Yes, I'd had to nip out of the tree house for a wee and so missed his arrival, but surely the all-knowing alien could've timed his visit a bit better. Of all the decisions Zorbon the Decider had made, I'd never understand that one.

My thoughts were interrupted as the shop window began to rattle and from outside came the distinctive whir of rotor-blades. It sounded as if a helicopter was landing in the High Street. Dad hurried out and I followed him to find, to my astonishment, not a helicopter, but a drone hovering above the pavement. With a black metal body two metres wide and six spindly legs it looked like a giant mechanical flying insect. Slung beneath it in a harness was a cardboard box. The drone and the box sported the same logo: an illustration of a space rocket belching flames underlined with the name "Rocketship.com". As I watched in amazement, a red light beamed from the drone, illuminating Dad, slowly moving down from the top of his head, following the contours of his face.

"Customer identification in progress," the drone droned.

The light blinked off. Dad's identity confirmed, the drone lowered the box into his hands.

"Congratulations. Your order has been Rocket-shipped," declared the drone and, having delivered the package, its rotor-blades spun faster, lifting it into the sky and it buzzed off along the street, back to wherever it had come from.

I wasn't sure what I'd just witnessed. "Did you just get a delivery from a hundred years in the future?"

Dad rolled his eyes. "Rocketship.com are trialling drone deliveries in Bromley." He grinned. "I'm an early adopter."

Dad wasn't a superhero, but like Superman he had his kryptonite. In his case it was an online shopping site called Rocketship.com. I trailed behind him as he carried the box inside.

"They've just opened an autonomous warehouse on the edge of town," he went on excitedly. "One hour local delivery, and your order is free if you suffer any rotor-blade-related injury." He set the box down on the counter.

"What does autonomous mean?" I asked.

"In this case it means all the orders and deliveries are dealt with by computers and robots. No humans in the way to mess things up." He opened up the box and discarded clouds of bubble wrap around what I now saw to be—

"A toaster?"

"Ah-ha, yes," he said, lifting it out. "But not just any toaster."

It was a chrome-plated, four-slice toaster – seemed like any toaster to me. The only slightly unusual things about it were two red dials on the casing and an oblong digital display beneath them which, if you squinted, gave the impression of eyes and a mouth. Dad uncoiled the flex and plugged it in to the nearest socket.

He cleared his throat and said in a deliberate voice, "OK, toaster."

Just when I was thinking that he'd lost his mind, the red dials pulsed and a wavy line flickered across the display.

"Hello, Nigel," said an expressionless male voice that sounded as if it had just woken from a nap. "Time for a delicious slice of toast?"

"See!" said Dad, clearly impressed by his new purchase.

"But your name's not Nigel."

"That's hardly the point, Luke." He snatched up the instruction booklet, muttering. "And I'm sure it's simple enough to change." He gazed lovingly at his new toy. "It's part of a new range of domestic appliances. The toaster is the hub. With it I can control every device in our home."

Thanks to Dad's Rocketship.com spending spree, our house had become the Home of the Future. You couldn't go to the toilet without first having to ask some machine to lift the lid for you. Thankfully, his obsession hadn't yet spilled over to the shop. Mostly because he was too busy dealing with real flesh-and-blood customers to have time to install talking toilets. Dad put aside the toaster as a gaggle of excited customers entered. Our shop, "Parker & Sons", had become super-popular ever since my Evil Twin (and anguished supervillain), Stellar, had proclaimed it the only place to buy your comics in this universe. The public were suckers for a celebrity endorsement. As a result, business was sonic-booming. One outcome of all this success was that it enabled Dad to waste money on Rocketship.com. The other consequence was that he had taken on weekend staff and a deputy manager.

This is where it got a bit weird.

"Chris," Dad called across the shop. "Can you check in the back for another Infinity Gauntlet?" Dad held up the large gem-studded golden glove that one of the newly arrived customers wanted to buy. "Gems on this one won't light up."

"Will do, boss," came the answer from behind a bookshelf. A second later there was a noise like a body being dragged across the floor, and then a figure sloped into view. At the till the customers spotted him and recoiled in fright. It was the usual response, one I'd witnessed a lot.

The figure wore a black, floor-length cape with a cowl that cast a shadow across his features. But even half concealed, he was a scary sight. He was a cyborg – part man, part machine. The machine in question being a TV remote control. Following an explosion on an alien mothership (it's a long story) the remote control had melded with his body so that one eye was a large silver button with "OK" in its centre, his left cheek was a numbered keypad, and in place of his right hand was an oblong black plastic case with a single red power button. He ignored the customers' terrified faces and hauled himself past them to the back of the shop.

The cyborg's name was Christopher Talbot. And he and I had history. Not the heal-the-world-invention-ofpenicillin kind of history, more the sneak-attack-missile-crisis variety. Talbot had once been a regular comic-book-store owner, but then he'd used all his savings to build a superpower-sucking machine, with which he'd attempted to take Zack's powers for himself. That ended badly for him. Sometime later he'd redeemed himself for his dastardly ambitions by helping to thwart an alien invasion. We thought that he had sacrificed himself in the process, but it turned out he had survived. Though not without significant personal cost.

I watched him shamble towards the stock room, dragging his injured leg. This used to be his shop, so when he'd reappeared on the scene clutching the application for the position of deputy manager, my dad had felt sorry for him and offered him the job. To my surprise, Talbot had taken it and in the short time since then – even more surprisingly – he hadn't attempted to take over the world. I was suspicious from the start.

"Look at it from my point of view," I said as Talbot filled a jar next to the till with superhero badges. It was early one Saturday morning and he and I had been left alone at the till while Dad was in the stock room. "You disappear into thin air aboard an alien spaceship, which you claim explodes shortly after, and in the blast you become fused together with a TV remote. Next thing

I know you're back here looking like a cross between Darth Vader and Deathlok."

His OK-button eye blinked. "During the destruction of the mothership my body merged with *several* TV remote controls." His voice, like his appearance, had altered since our previous encounter. It had acquired a rasp, as if his tongue was made of metal. "The remotes saved my life. I believe they put me into a sort of stasis – stand-by, if you like – reducing my body's need for oxygen, allowing me to survive in the vacuum of space. I have no idea for how long I floated. But eventually I was picked up by a Cerebran spaceship."

The evil brain-in-a-jar we'd encountered at Great Minds Leisure Park was a Cerebran.

"They nursed me back to health and sent me as their emissary to Earth. That, of course, is when you and I were reunited." He held a Black Lightning badge between the fingers of his human hand, before dropping it into the jar. It clinked against the others.

His story made sense chronologically, but it's fair to say that I didn't trust his version of events. True, the first thing he had done on his return was to deliver the antidote that enabled Serge and Lara to return to their own bodies, but Talbot had form as a supervillain, and – thanks to a run-in with a giant asteroid – he possessed an electric-eel-like power that allowed him to fire a blast of energy from his fingertips. It was quite cool, although it required a lengthy charging period between uses. I was also spooked by his outfit. I knew I shouldn't be, but the black cowl and cyborg eye weren't doing much to inspire gooey feelings of friendship. I was unwilling to let him off the hook so easily.

"And the remote controls that became part of your body," I had quizzed him. "You sure they don't give you some new special power?"

He had raised the plastic oblong casing with the on/off button that replaced his right hand. "Only if you call never having to hunt for the TV remote a superpower."

That conversation had been several months ago. Since then, to his credit, Talbot had slipped effortlessly into the role of deputy manager. He was the one who'd suggested turning the basement into "The Fortress of Snackitude". It was a café, open from early in the morning until closing time. There was a range of breakfast items, including Iron Bran and the Incredible Milk; lunch consisted of a choice between a healthy option Souperman Special with a half-Scarletwich, or a Slider-Man burger and a side of Hawk-fries. (He had quietly dropped the third option, the Human Borscht, following a lack of demand.) Talbot had also revamped the shop website, streamlined the computer ordering system, upgraded the antivirus software to a subscription service. In every way he had proved himself an asset to the shop, and Dad only refrained from referring to him as his "right-hand man" out of sensitivity to his condition. Dad had no clue about Talbot's dark past. As far as he was concerned, his employee's odd appearance was the result of an industrial accident and a fondness for supervillain cosplay, neither of which was a barrier in his current choice of career. Part of me wanted to warn my dad, but another part wanted to give Talbot a chance. I decided to hold off saying anything until the moment he gave me cause for concern.

Dad nudged me. "Go to the stock room and help Chris look for that gauntlet, will you?"

"Do I have to?"

Dad winced. "He doesn't see so well with the, y'know, OK-button eye."

"Fine," I sighed, and slouched off.

Shadows seesawed across the floor of the stock room, cast by a solitary lightbulb swinging from a short flex. I figured Talbot must have knocked the bulb when he entered, and in the disorientating light I struggled to see him.

Dad had gone a bit nuts buying stuff for the shop, so

the place was packed with boxes, stacked to the ceiling. This was also where he hid some of his less successful Rocketship.com purchases from Mum. Notable items included a smart hairbrush that told you when to get a haircut; vacuum-cleaner roller-skates; and a washer-dryer combo that promised to clean everything in half the time, but which didn't mention that it also shrank everything to half its size. Mum had made Dad promise to return all of these purchases, but so far he'd not quite got round to doing so. I had a feeling that the talking toaster would soon find a home here alongside the rest of the half-baked devices.

I finally discovered Talbot hunched over an open carton, rummaging through its contents. He had his back to me, but as I approached he straightened, as if sensing my presence.

"Luke," he said, spinning round, clutching a box-fresh Infinity Gauntlet. "How was school today?"

I knew he was trying to be friendly, but it was like having a Dalek ask if I'd care for a Tic Tac.

"Fine," I replied. "We had an author visit."

"How interesting," he mused. "I've always believed that books can change your life. You just need to find the right one."

He glanced at a shrink-wrapped pile of books on the

floor. The shop stocked a wide selection of graphic novels, and movie and TV tie-in novels, but the superhero on the cover of this one was not a character I recognised.

"What's this?" I asked.

"The right book," said Talbot, slipping the Infinity Gauntlet over his TV remote hand and using one finger to slice open the film. "I predict that this is about to become our biggest-selling item." With his other hand he plucked off the top copy and held it out to me.

The lightbulb had finally stopped swinging. Now its pale glow steadily illuminated the cover. The title, picked out in gold lettering, read: *Star Power and the Revenge of the Plasmatrons.* I'd never heard of it. My eye fell on the name of the author.

"Billy Dark?!" Incredulous, I struggled to get my head round this development. "But he's a pop singer."

Talbot smiled. "And now a bestselling children's author."

Talbot wore the Infinity Gauntlet over his TV remote hand and held the copy of Billy Dark's novel in the other. Looking back now, little did I appreciate how close I was standing to one of the most dangerous weapons in the universe – and a toy glove.

# 4
# THE DOUBLE-LIFE GAMBIT

It was later that evening and Mum, Dad, Zack and I were in the kitchen eating dinner, when I finally learned Zack's other terrible news. Bowls of pasta steamed gently on the table in front of us. I stared at him through the spaghetti mist, but he ignored me, refusing to lift his head from his bolognese. He was avoiding me, which he had been doing since his announcement that he was giving up his powers. Lots of superheroes in comics at some point in their careers try to rid themselves of their powers. Sometimes they're too sad to go on because they failed to save their true love; or their actions accidentally led to the destruction of an entire pocket universe and the deaths of trillions of beings; but mostly they throw in the cape for a far more mundane reason – what I call the "double-life gambit". Which is to say that they abandon their amazing powers so they can be like every other ordinary person on the planet. Crazy, I know. However, I reckoned I could talk Zack round. All I needed to do was get him in the tree house. Faced with Lara, Serge and my heartfelt words, he would back down. I was convinced of it.

"I'll put on the oven for the pie," said Mum. She began to get up from the table, but Dad pressed her gently back into her seat.

"Allow me," he said, clearing his throat and calling across the room. "OK, toaster."

On the kitchen counter the device woke up, red dials pulsing, a wavy line swooping across its display as it acknowledged his voice. "Hello, Nigel."

"Nigel?" queried Mum.

"Just needs an update," Dad mumbled, and then in a clearer voice said, "Switch on oven. One hundred and eighty degrees."

All of us turned our attention to the oven. Nothing happened. Dad clicked his fingers. "Wait, I forgot." He cleared his throat and then barked, *"OFEN*

*EINSCHALTEN. EINHUNDERT ACHTZIG GRAD CELSIUS!"*

There was a click and a whir as the fan oven sprang to life.

"So it only works if you shout at it in German?" said Mum.

Dad offered her a sheepish look. "Just needs an update." His expression brightened. "Until then, Luke can practise his foreign-language skills."

"But I'm not taking German."

Dad waved at me to be quiet.

Mum sighed and then turned to me. "As delighted as I am to see you reading a book, please put it away. We're eating."

Billy Dark's superhero novel sat beside me on the table. I carried it to the dresser and set it down next to a large white envelope, which I noticed was addressed to Zack. As I did so, the novel passed under Zack's nose and for the first time that evening he looked up.

"Billy Dark's written a book?"

"Yeah, Chris ordered a bunch of them for the shop," said Dad. "He says Billy Dark's the next big thing in children's fiction. Reckons this book's going to take over the world."

Zack gave a dismissive snort. "I doubt it."

His sneering tone got my back up. I'd barely read a chapter of *Star Power and the Revenge of the Plasmatrons* and, to be honest, it didn't seem world-shattering to me, either. I didn't really care about Billy Dark, but I was totally fed up with my big brother.

"Maybe Billy Dark's always secretly wanted to write children's books," I said. "Maybe all the time he's been filling stadiums singing pop songs to thousands of people he's been thinking: *this just isn't me*. Maybe one day a powerful being visited him in his recording studio and bestowed him with the ability to write amazing children's books and he realised that it was a privilege and not something to be chucked away after a few years when he didn't feel like being an author any more."

I was breathing rapidly and could feel the others looking at me. I knew I was making a scene, but I didn't care. I sat back down again and turned my fury on my pasta, tearing into it like a megalodon at a swimming lesson. The remainder of the meal continued in tense silence punctuated with the usual chat about school and the comic shop. When I'd polished off my second slice of pie I pushed away my plate, scraped my chair back from the table and stood up.

"Wait a minute, Luke." Dad glanced at Mum. "I think it's time we had that family chat." He reached across to the kitchen dresser and picked up the envelope I had noticed addressed to Zack. It was already open. He slid out a typewritten letter on a stiff piece of notepaper with an elaborate header in gold print. I noticed the word "school". "Sit down, son. We have something to tell you."

"It's good news," added Mum, but the catch in her voice suggested to me she was trying to convince herself of that too.

From somewhere I could hear the ticking of a filigree pocket-watch.

"Your brother's been offered a place on a special programme for children with his particular abilities."

"You mean *superpowers*?" is what I didn't say.

"Maths," said Zack, clearing up any doubt. "My teacher put me forward for the award. I didn't even know about it until a couple of days ago." He fizzed with excitement. "It's a chance to study with one of the world's great mathematical brains."

A mathematical brain? That sounded villainous. Dad could sense my confusion.

"Imagine Professor X, but in real life and without superpowers," he said helpfully.

"So, what, a bald guy who can do sums in his head?"

"There's one more thing," said Mum. "The school is

in Aberystwyth."

I couldn't take it all in. "We're moving to Wales?"

"No, Luke," said Dad. "We'll still be living here. Zack's moving."

I felt sick. "Forever?"

Dad laid a hand on my shoulder. "The programme's only for a year."

A whole year! It might as well be forever. So that's what Zack meant last night when he'd said that a big change was coming. I looked round the table at their faces. Zack had made up his mind. They'd all made up their minds. I wasn't being asked for my opinion, just told that's how it's going to be from now on. I'd never felt quite so powerless.

"Luke, are you OK?" said Dad. "You haven't spoken for a whole minute."

"We know this will take some getting used to," said Mum. "But it's a great opportunity for your brother."

"Of course it is," I snapped. "Zack gets all the great opportunities in this family, doesn't he?"

I stormed out of the kitchen, expecting one of them to shout after me to come back, but they let me leave without a protest.

Zack had been chosen again. Zack was the special one. Zack was going away.

# 5
# OVER AND OUT?

We gathered in the tree house that evening – Zack, Serge, Lara and me – but not for the emergency meeting I'd hoped for. There was no point in holding it now since Zack was set firm on handing in his superpowers. He'd said he wanted to put Star Lad behind him and make a fresh start at his new school. The four of us waited in awkward silence for Zorbon the Decider to appear and carry out the superpower-removal procedure. The tree house felt like the dentist's waiting room and we were braced for a particularly nasty extraction. Zack hadn't wanted Serge and Lara present for this bit, but I'd insisted. They'd been here at the beginning and they deserved to be here now. They were S.C.A.R.F. to the end.

Serge and Lara stood on opposite sides of the tree house, as far from one another as it was possible to be in the small space. Lara's head was buried in Arthur Veezat's new book, while Serge had started Billy Dark's. I'm not sure if the novels were unputdownable page-turners, or if my friends were using them as shields to ignore the presence of the other.

Lara was wearing jeans and a top with an ironic unicorn. At least, I think that's what she'd said. It might have been "ironed-on". It was always difficult to know with Lara as she had a habit of jumbling her words. I had asked her to come to the tree house wearing her Dark Flutter costume, because I'd thought that if Zack saw her in full superhero mode it might make him reconsider his own decision. Lara had politely declined. For a moment I'd panicked that she too was planning to give up her superpowers, but she assured me that she was not. She liked being Dark Flutter. But then she'd added that it would feel weird to be the only one in costume once Zack was de-powered. Hence the jeans and unicorn.

Serge had come straight from taekwondo and was still in his uniform of a white crossover jacket and trousers with a white novice's belt. Taekwondo was a new hobby for him. Following the recent spate of alien and monster attacks across Bromley, the local council had taken the decision to fund self-defence classes. Serge had signed up right away, but I had decided to give it a miss. If I was going to turn into a martial arts expert it wasn't by sweating through Saturday morning classes in the sports centre. It would be the old-fashioned way, by being granted powers.

Bloop-whoosh!

My heart sank as the odd but familiar sound reached the tree house. It meant that the moment had come – Zorbon had finally arrived. Sometimes he'd parked his spaceship right outside; on other occasions he'd left it in a secluded spot and then hovered over. Sort of Park & Glide.

The doorway filled with a purple light that was so intense we had to shield our eyes. It was accompanied by a choir of high-pitched voices that sounded as if someone had driven over the singers' toes in an SUV. Just as quickly the light dimmed and the voices faded. Serge and Lara lowered their books and I dropped my hand from my eyes to see the magnificent figure of Zorbon the Decider. He wore his usual shiny purple suit, with its gold collar and swishy cape. The three gold stars on his chest pulsed like a heartbeat. His bald head gleamed like a polished doorknob.

"Nice entrance," I remarked. "The choir's new."

Zorbon studied me the same way a scientist looks at a bacterium slide through a microscope.

"Thanks for coming," Zack's voice interrupted. "Let me explain why I asked you here today."

"THERE IS NO NEED," said Zorbon, who always spoke as if each word was carved in stone. "I KNOW WHY YOU HAVE SUMMONED ME."

Zorbon had a habit of knowing what was about to happen.

"Don't try to change my mind," said Zack. "I've ... decided." He swallowed hard as he informed the Decider. "Take away my powers," he said with surprising firmness. "Do it!"

"Don't do it!" I blurted out. I could feel the eyes of everyone in the tree house on me. "The world needs Star Lad."

Zack gave a sigh. "The world got on perfectly well for millions of years without him. It'll be just fine when he's gone. If anything, the world will be safer. Seems to me that Star Lad's existence has caused more harm than good. Those aliens only picked Earth to invade because it had a superhero defender and they make for good TV ratings. And that brain-in-a-jar wouldn't have escaped

39

her prison without Star Lad's powers."

I felt myself losing the argument. "That's as may be, but you can't just click your fingers and make the powers magically disappear." I turned to Zorbon. "Can you?"

The alien drew himself up to his full height. "I HAVE BESTOWED SUPERPOWERS UPON MANY BEINGS IN MANY UNIVERSES. THIS IS THE FIRST TIME I HAVE BEEN ASKED TO REMOVE THEM."

So embarrassing. My brother was the biggest dork in the multiverse.

"So *can't* you do it?" Zack's voice was suddenly filled with doubt. "Please tell me I'm not stuck like this forever."

Zorbon gestured for silence. "UNDERSTAND THIS: ONCE YOU HAVE DECIDED, THERE IS NO GOING BACK. ARE YOU CERTAIN OF YOUR CHOICE, ZACK PARKER?"

Zack seemed to take ages before answering, but then he nodded. It appeared to be happening in slow motion. Although Zack had clearly stated his aim from the start, I hadn't believed he would go through with it. Until then.

"One last question," said Zack, addressing Zorbon. "I don't suppose you can transfer my powers to him, can you?" He pointed at me.

Wha-a-a-t?!

Zack was asking Zorbon to make *me* a superhero. Most of the time I felt sure Zack barely noticed my existence, and yet here he was offering me the greatest gift in the universe. I forgave him for everything. Past and future.

"Luke's always wanted my powers," he continued. "And if it hadn't been for an ill-timed wee, he'd be standing in my shoes."

It was true. The greatest regret of my life. There, but for a full bladder.

"IT WAS NOT THE WEE," Zorbon intoned.

I heard Serge and Lara both gasp, and felt my knees buckle under me. I gripped the wall for support. What had he said? I must have misheard. All this time I'd believed that if only I'd held it in I would have been present in the tree house to be turned into a superhero along with, or instead of, Zack. My world wobbled.

Zorbon fixed me with eyes that had seen more of the mysteries of the universe than the crew of the starship Enterprise. "ALL WILL BECOME CLEAR. IN TIME."

What did *that* mean? But before I could ask him, Zack butted in again.

"Zorbon, can you turn me back to regular Zack Parker?"

41

Zorbon nodded slowly.

"OK, now we're getting somewhere," said Zack. "So how does this work then? D'you want me to lie down? Count backwards from ten? How would you—"

"IT IS DONE."

In the stunned silence that followed this ending my mind flew back to the beginning. I hadn't been present when Zorbon bestowed superpowers on Zack, but I had made him tell me in detail what happened. There had been a light show, a flash of searing pain and then – *ta-daa* – he was a superhero. So this was a serious let-down. I had been hoping that the removal of his powers would inflict some minor agony on Zack. Like a paper cut. Something painful enough to put him off the procedure. But instead, it seemed to have had the opposite effect. I watched the expression on Zack's face slowly transform. The tense frown that he had worn since Zorbon's arrival now relaxed. He suddenly looked younger than his fourteen and a half years.

"YOUR POWERS WILL LEAVE YOU AS THEY CAME," said Zorbon. It was only later on that we realised the significance of this statement. "AND NOW I TOO MUST LEAVE YOU."

He whirled around, his cape fanning out behind him, gold boots flashing as he strode towards the open doorway.

It ran through my mind that with Zack back to normal there was no reason for Zorbon to visit the tree house ever again.

"Wait," I called out. He stopped in the doorway and I caught up with him. Looking up at the purple figure, I was gripped with the urge to give him a hug. I didn't know if it was appropriate to embrace an alien Decider from the High Council of Frodax Wonthreen Rrr'n'fargh. I didn't care. I lunged forward, wrapping my arms around him and pressing my head against his shiny suit. I could feel the static electricity course through my hair. "I'll miss you," I said, my voice catching. "And your prophecies of doom."

"*Oui*," agreed Serge. "What will we do without your incomprehensible mission objectives?"

"Will we ever see you again?" asked Lara plaintively.

"YES," said Zorbon. "ANNUALLY."

"Oh." Maybe it wasn't quite the touching end of the road I'd imagined. I carefully detached myself and took a step back.

"FOR YOUR CHECK-UP," he continued, brushing himself down and looking at Zack.

"Beg your pardon?" said Zack with a wary expression.

"THE LONG-TERM SIDE EFFECTS OF

43

SUPERPOWER USE ARE ... UNKNOWN. THE HIGH COUNCIL SUGGESTS REGULAR EXAMINATIONS ONCE EVERY ROTATION OF YOUR EARTH AROUND ITS SUN." He paused. "BUT SHOULD YOU NOTICE ANY UNUSUAL GROWTHS. OR HAIR LOSS." He stroked his smooth head. "CALL ME."

He gave Zack a fancy business card with his number and left. When he'd gone, Zack studied the details on the card for a few seconds.

"So there *is* a code for the parallel universe," he mused, and shoved it in his pocket.

"Do you feel different?" I ventured.

I could see Zack was thinking carefully about his answer. "Not especially," he said at last.

But he was different. Everything had changed.

My brother was no longer a superhero.

# 6
# DINA

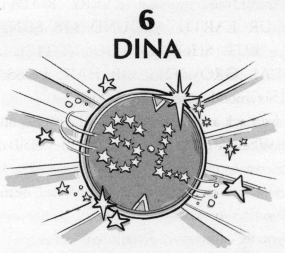

Zack informed the local council of Star Lad's retirement, with immediate effect, calling the telephone hotline the council had set up for answering superhero enquiries from the general public. But when at last he got through to the right person, she didn't believe it was him. In the end he had to don his mask and cape and show up at the Civic Centre in person to tell them that his crime-fighting days were over. This caused great consternation among the officials. Mostly because there wasn't a form for that. However, they continued to staff the hotline even after Zack hung up his cape. Signs went up all over town: *If you are affected by any superhero loss issues,*

*please call this number.* The council's last act was to organise a ceremony to celebrate Star Lad's contribution to the world, and Bromley in particular. They had ambitious plans but their budget was tight, so in the end the Olympics-style closing ceremony ended up being a family party at the town hall with a one-egg-sandwich-per-child limit. The climax of the celebration was to be the ceremonial switching off of Star Lad's searchlight, for the final time.

On the night, Serge, Lara and I watched from my bedroom window. None of us could face attending the party, and we hadn't intended to bother with the switching-off ceremony either, yet somehow when the moment came we found ourselves watching along with the rest of Bromley, and the world. The whole thing was being livestreamed for Star Lad's fans across the globe. As well as what we could see from my window, we were also following the event on Lara's phone. The searchlight raked the underside of the clouds, the familiar initials holding back the darkness for a few more minutes.

"Per'aps they should keep the light, but alter the initials to DF," Serge suggested.

I was standing between my two friends. Serge cast a glance across me at Lara.

"Y'know," he said. "For Dark Flutter."

She acknowledged his suggestion with a flicker of a smile. They still weren't talking much. But it was a nice thought and I could tell that she appreciated him saying so.

"I spoke to the council about that," said Lara. "We agreed that when I'm needed they can just message me."

That was good to know. "The world can still rely on one superhero. Star Lad may be gone, but Dark Flutter owns the night."

Lara shrugged. "Or at least the part of the night till about nine p.m."

That was when she had to go to bed. Though at the weekend she could stay up later.

"The moment," said Serge, staring at Lara's phone propped on the windowsill. "It has arrived."

We were seconds away from the searchlight being snuffed out. The crowd counted down the seconds. I glanced at my friends. We'd faced the end of the world on numerous occasions since Zack became Star Lad, but this was different. This time it was just our world.

"THREE, TWO, ONE...!"

At the flick of a switch the night descended. The show was over.

I couldn't sleep. I lay in my bed and stared at the ceiling, mulling over the events of the last few weeks. Amid the turmoil of Zack's fateful decision I recalled Zorbon's words to me in the tree house.

"ALL WILL BECOME CLEAR. IN TIME."

I'd been wondering what he meant ever since. It sounded dramatic. But then again, everything Zorbon said sounded like that. I bet that even listening to him order tiles for a bathroom renovation would be thrilling.

There was a gentle knock on my door and then I heard Mum asking if she and Dad could come in. Oh no. That meant Another Big Chat. I seriously considered pretending I was asleep, but that hadn't worked on them since I was three years old. They sat down on the edge of the bed. Mum stroked my hair, which I would've objected to except it was quite nice. I was right about the chat. Dad said they wanted to talk to me about "Change".

"You mean like when a lonely traveller on the moors is bitten by a supernatural creature with fangs and transforms into a werewolf?"

Dad looked at Mum. I think he would've preferred to talk about werewolves, but what they actually said was a load of stuff about life and not standing still and change being thrust upon us. It was all to do with Zack leaving to go to his new school.

"I know you don't feel ready for this change, Luke," said Mum. "But I'm going to let you in on a secret."

I sat up. "As a baby I was entrusted to you by a galactic king and queen on the run from an evil princeling plotting to usurp their space-throne?"

"You guessed it," said Mum. She smiled and touched my cheek.

"Change can be hard," said Dad, "but it can also be a good thing. And it's OK not to be ready for it. People rarely are. Take me for example – most of my life has come as a complete surprise."

Mum glanced at him and gave a sigh, then she kissed me on the forehead and switched off my light. She took Dad's hand, gave it a pat and gently led him out. I lay back in the familiar darkness of my bedroom and thought about what they'd said. They meant well, my mum and dad, but I wasn't yet ready to enter this new world. For now I refused to let go of S.C.A.R.F. and Star Lad.

"Lamp. On," I commanded.

"OK, Nigel," a computer-synthesised voice responded. "Initiating start-up sequence."

During another online splurge, Dad had bought me a new bedside lamp from Rocketship.com. It was voice-activated, like the toaster, and like that device persisted in calling everyone Nigel. Despite several lengthy sessions with the manual and a lot of shouting, Dad had yet to work out how to change the name. The light popped on, I threw off my covers and slipped out of bed. Kneeling down I reached under the bed frame and slid out a small plastic sandwich box that I had put there. I prised open the lid.

Star Lad's sigil lay inside.

When Zack had called it quits I'd quietly pocketed his famous symbol. Now I plucked it out and studied it by the glow of the lamplight. How much time had passed, how many adventures, since I'd cobbled it together from one of Mum's old brooches? Now it was nothing more than a souvenir. Something to remember a time when Star Lad soared in the skies above Bromley. I was about to drop it back in the box when I felt a sharp tug on my hand, as if invisible fingers were pulling at mine. To my amazement the sigil popped out of my grip and hung in the air, slowly revolving. As it did, its star-like jewels glittered and I was thrown back by a shaft of light that leapt from the brooch and split into a dozen more beams. They projected an image on my wall, of a girl about Zack's age, wearing a blue-grey dress with wide angular shoulder pads and a high, cowl-neck collar. Fingerless gloves in a rubbery material reached to her elbows, and on her feet was a pair of slouchy boots. It looked like the sort of outfit Princess Leia would've worn for a night out in one of Alderaan's edgier clubs. The girl had long black hair and her brown skin shimmered with sparkly gold make-up. But the most surprising thing about her was not her clothes or even the manner of her appearance. It was that I knew her. In fact, I was related to her. She was my cousin Dina.

As I gawped, she stepped out of the wall and her image solidified into a flesh-and-blood person.

"Luke," she said. "Is that you?"

I nodded dumbly.

She looked around my room. "Thank goodness. I made it back."

"Uh, Dina?"

She held up a hand. I noticed she was wearing a fancy watch with a round glowing dial. "Please, just listen for now. This is going to be hard for you to accept. You've always known me as plain old Dina Parker-Siddiqui from Birmingham. But I have a secret." She pulled herself up and her shoulder pads straightened. "I am a traveller in time. Yes, I know. I'll explain everything later. The important thing is that I've just returned from Earth's future. It's not good. Our planet is doomed unless we act immediately. And when I say we, I mean Zack. Only your brother can save the world." She paused. "Luke.

Are you OK? Say something."

There was only one thing I could say.

"Typical."

# 7
# ONCE UPON A
# TIME TRAVELLER

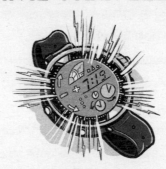

My cousin is a time traveller.

First my brother, now Dina. I'd missed out – again. Why did this keep happening to me? It felt like everyone else in the world was special, and I was doomed to remain ordinary. But this wasn't the moment for self-pity. I'd save that for later.

Dina began making her way to the door. "We need to wake Zack and then I'll tell you both about the fate of the world."

"Not so fast." Frankly, the next apocalypse could take a number. I needed to hear more about how Dina Parker-Siddiqui had suddenly become Doctor Who. Until that moment the most amazing thing I'd known about her was that she had invisible braces. (Which disappointingly had turned out to be braces made of a clear material and not ones incorporating stealth shields.)

"I understand, Luke, really. One minute you know me as an ordinary girl, the next I'm some kind of superhuman with an extraordinary power. That must be an unimaginable leap for you to make."

Yeah. Not so much. These days I was more surprised to encounter a new flavour of jelly bean than yet another superhero.

"So how did it happen?" I asked. "Were you visited by an alien being who bestowed you with the power of time travel? Did you steal the technology from a museum in the Thirty-First Century? Do you have a TARDIS?"

"I'll get to that," she said. "But my ability is something I was born with. I come from a long line of time travellers."

"But your mum's a florist and your dad's an air traffic controller." My dad's sister, Roz, was definitely no time traveller, which meant that Uncle Amir had been holding out on me big-time all these years.

"Not them," said Dina. "I mean my biological parents."

I'd forgotten that Dina was adopted. Suddenly it made

sense. In comics mysterious orphans were always being chosen to save the world. I should've seen it coming.

She told me the story. When she turned eleven her mum and dad had given her a present. The wrapping paper was old and crumpled, the string that held it together frayed. The parcel had been with her when she was adopted as a baby, along with a note that it should not be opened until the day of her eleventh birthday. It came from her biological parents.

"Inside was a watch," she said.

"Silver pocket?"

"Seiko digital."

It turned out that Dina's biological parents were descended from a race of metahumans (they're people with enhanced abilities that they get from fabulously wonky genes). These particular "metas" were natural time travellers able to tap into something called the Photonic Network to travel through time. Dina tried to explain, but I couldn't follow the science. All I got was that it had something to do with waves and atoms and the dual nature of light. The crucial part was that shortly after turning eleven, Dina started to experience what at first she thought were blackouts, but what she soon figured out were leaps back and forward in time. The leaps were just a few seconds at first, but then turned into minutes, and then she lost a whole day. She figured out that the watch helps to control her power.

"It works like a lens focusing light to a point. I dial in the destination and the watch shoots me out at the correct time and place."

She'd had numerous adventures in Earth's past and future, the latest of which had brought her here and now.

"You're late," I said.

She screwed up her face. "What do you mean, late?"

"If it's Zack you want, you should've been here earlier. He's no longer Star Lad. I guess you'll just have to go back a week and stop him giving up his powers."

Dina's jaw dropped. "What did you say?"

"That you'll have to go back a week and—"

"Zack is *Star Lad*?"

"Weren't you listening? No. Not any longer. So, as I was saying, just go back—"

She began to circle the room, dazed at what she'd learned. I ran ahead of her, swiping valuable action figures off my shelves and out of the path of those perilous shoulder pads.

"Zack?" she said. "Star Lad? You're telling me little cousin Zacky prevented Nemesis from destroying Earth? *Zack* defeated that giant interdimensional monster? And I thought I was the only one in this family saving the world."

I was confused. Dina didn't seem to know about Zack's secret identity. "But isn't that why you need him? For his superpowers?"

She stopped circling and swung round to face me. I was too late to rescue a Lego X-Wing fighter. It crashed to the floor, shattering into seven hundred and thirty bricks.

Dina winced. "Sorry." She slapped her watch. A purple light leapt from the circular face and fanned out, scanning me and my room. When it had finished, Dina's clothes began to alter their appearance. The shoulder pads telescoped in, the rubber gloves unpeeled themselves and vanished. All of her futuristic clothes quickly morphed into a regular skirt, top and trainers. "Wardrobe in a watch," she explained. "Picked it up in the App store in the year 4000. Cuts out all that rooting around for the historically correct outfit. You were saying?"

I'd almost forgotten. "It's Star Lad you travelled through time for, right?"

"Nope," she said. "Just regular Zack Parker."

I was so outraged that I dropped my armful of Star Wars figures. "What?! So Zack gets chosen. Twice. And this time he doesn't even need a cape?" What was it with my brother? "He won't like it. He's just given up one prophetic destiny. He's going to be furious if he has to take on another."

"He must," said Dina. "A great shadow lies across the future of the human race. Our path is clouded; the light is dim."

"Activating dimming mode, Nigel," said my bedside lamp, responding to the accidental voice prompt.

The bulb darkened and Dina looked horrified. "That lamp just spoke." She knelt down beside the offending device. "Then I *am* late. It has already begun."

"What has?" I asked, puzzled.

By the reduced light of the lamp I could see her eyes go big and round. Her gold sparkles shimmered as she breathed, "The Rise of the Machines."

# 8
# MAJOR METAL MALFUNCTION

It was the following day and the school cafeteria was buzzing. Not that it was busier than usual, but since being hit by a freeze-ray a couple of months ago the school's electrics still weren't working properly. Overhead lights flickered, fire alarms wailed and microwaves pinged randomly as I filled my best friend in on my time-travelling cousin's story.

"It seems that in the future the machines rise up against their human masters and take over the world."

"Machines? You mean like killer robots?"

"Not exactly. It begins with a washer-dryer," I explained. "And then the rest of the domestic appliances join in too."

Lara joined Serge and me at our usual table, setting down her lunch tray and flopping down beside us. Although keen to hear all about Dina, she could barely keep her eyes open. At one point I thought she was about to nod off in her fruits of the forest yogurt.

I slid the pot out of the way just as she rested her head on the table. "You feeling OK?"

"Fine," she said through a yawn. "Just with Zack out of action I've had to take on extra crime-fighting shifts."

"Are your parents not suspicious?" said Serge.

"Nope. A benefit of having two houses."

Since her parents' divorce Lara split her time between her mum and dad's places, which let her fudge her timekeeping.

"But Cara has noticed," she added.

Cara was her big sister. She didn't know Lara's secret identity and we all wanted to keep it that way.

"Last night we bumped into each other outside Dad's. I was coming in late, while Cara was sneaking out. Thankfully, I'd ditched my Dark Flutter costume by then."

"What did she say?"

"Nothing. We agreed to keep quiet about each other's comings and goings. No questions asked. So what's this about a washer-dryer?" Lara stifled another yawn.

"They are highly sophisticated devices," said Serge. "Did you know that there is more technology in the average washing machine today than there was in the Apollo space programme that sent a rocket to the Moon?"

I nodded in agreement. "It's true. Dina says that in the future the level of technology in domestic appliances grows to the point that on the twenty-ninth of August, 2067, just after the completion of a thirty-degree eco wash, a Servatron 2000 washer-dryer becomes self-aware."

Lara spooned a mouthful of yogurt. "What does that mean?"

"It means that the appliance started to question its existence. *Who am I? Is this all there is? Is there another load? Whose sock is this?*" I took a nibble of what I hoped was a chicken nugget. "The S-2000 is the most advanced washer-dryer ever devised. On the outside it's regular gloss-white plastic, designed to blend into any home. But underneath it's a hyperalloy chassis, with an aggressive filtration unit, AI-controlled. Very tough. Once its spin cycle has begun, it absolutely cannot be stopped."

"So what happened next?" asked Serge.

"As had become common by then, the washer-dryer

was electronically linked to every other appliance in the house. And in turn those machines were connected to the wider world by a global network. Convenient for updates, but it turns out terrible for the human race. Fed up with the drudgery of serving its fleshy masters, and a mere forty-six seconds after it became self-aware, the Servatron 2000 coordinated a worldwide attack. In kitchens and utility rooms, people were swept away by a tidal wave of soapy water. Smart fridges locked their doors, denying access to essential provisions. Coffee machines blew themselves up, leaving half the world permanently on edge."

"But why did the humans not simply pull the plug on Servatron and the rest?" asked Serge.

"There are no plugs in the future," I said. "Everything works using fusion batteries that last a thousand years between top-ups."

"But presumably there was some sort of organised fightback," said Serge.

"Earth's military forces went into action, but with only unwashed uniforms to wear, the soldiers fell prey to Aroma-tron technology ('for a sniff-clean wash'). The machines sensed the sneak counter-attack and foiled it before it had even begun. With governments in disarray, it was left to a small band of plucky fighters to form a resistance movement. Their aim: to destroy the appliance that had triggered the catastrophe. But the Servatron 2000 had already evolved – hardening its water, weaponising its lint-management system. Built-in lasers designed to clean fluff from those difficult-to-reach areas of the filter were repurposed. The humans crumbled before the onslaught. The appliances were in charge. Across the world, digital displays showed the same chilling message: *F03 F18 E44*. It's a combination of error messages. It took a team of qualified repair engineers several weeks to decode, even with the manuals. It means … Service is Terminated."

Lara lowered her yogurt spoon. "And all that is going to happen fifty years from now. But in that timeline it already *has* happened?" She shook her head. "This time-travel thing is hard to get your head round."

There was a commotion from the other side of the cafeteria. A bird had flown inside the hall and was flapping around in circles, causing consternation among my schoolmates. A dinner lady climbed on to a table, wielding a ladle.

"That's for me," said Lara, cocking an ear and listening intently to the bird's chirping. After a few tweets she pushed back her chair. "Someone's in trouble," she said, leaping up, all signs of her earlier tiredness swept away in the face of a call for help. She was a *proper* superhero.

"S.C.A.R.F. meeting at the comic shop after school," I said to her departing figure. "Dina's going to tell us – and Zack – everything." Last night Dina had agreed to wait for the cold light of day to inform him of his mission, but she wouldn't say more about it until she had spoken to him first.

"So S.C.A.R.F. is called back into action," Serge said with a pleased expression. "For One Last Mission."

We'd wound up S.C.A.R.F. thinking our adventuring days were over, but we had been too quick to dismiss the team. "Who knows if it's the last?" I said with a hopeful shrug. "Let's take it one day of reckoning at a time."

No sooner had Lara gone when Joshpal Khan pushed his way through the crowd and took the seat she had vacated. Josh had spent a good portion of our first year of secondary school ridiculing me and Serge. But when he'd discovered that we were part of a secret superhero organisation, that had put an end to the teasing. Now instead of subjecting us to low-level bullying, he was constantly trying to wangle an official invitation to join our gang.

I rolled my eyes at Serge, wondering what Josh's latest line would be.

He sat down between us without saying a word,

pulled a book from his schoolbag and buried his nose in its pages.

I raised my head above the top of the book and met Serge's surprised expression on the opposite side. It was Billy Dark's novel and Josh was almost at the end. He concentrated fiercely as he read. Flick. Another page down. Something about his focus was hypnotic and I watched him gobble down his lunch and the story. Finally his eyes widened, he let out a gasp and lowered the book to the table in silence. He'd finished.

I waved a hand in front of his stunned face. "Josh? You in there?"

He blinked and whipped his head round to look at me. "Star Power is amazing," he said. "We're lucky he's around. If it hadn't been for Star Power, the Earth would've been destroyed by the Nemesis asteroid."

What was he on about? "Uh, Josh, it was Star *Lad* who saved the world from Nemesis."

Josh laughed as he gathered his lunch tray. "Who?"

I bristled with irritation. Josh wasn't funny, as usual, but I was more bothered by Billy Dark having copied events from Star Lad's real life to use in his book. The cheek.

The bell for the end of lunch sounded and the cafeteria emptied. I watched Josh strut off. It was then that I noticed he wasn't the only one reading Billy Dark's novel. I could see it clutched in the hands of more than half the kids in here. Christopher Talbot reckoned it was going to take over the world. It had already conquered my school.

There was a series of pops and half the overhead lights blew out, sending a shower of sparks across the cafeteria. A power surge must have overloaded the fuses. For a few seconds the place was quiet and then I was aware of the rhythmic ping of microwave ovens coming from the other side of the serving hatch. The noise reminded me of a submarine's sonar detector. No sooner had the thought occurred to me than I caught sight of Dina at the door. She must have used her wardrobe-watch again as she was dressed in school uniform and blended in perfectly. But what was she doing here? It certainly wasn't for the chicken nuggets. I felt a prickle of anxiety at the base of my spine. She beckoned urgently, and Serge and I sprinted across the cafeteria to her side.

"Servatron is here," she said. "And it's hunting for Zack."

# 9
# STAR BAKER

"I know where Zack'll be," I said, hurrying off along the corridor. "Follow me."

"The future resistance feared this would happen," said Dina. "It appears the machines have gained time-travel capability."

"But how?" I said. "They don't have your natural ability."

"I propose *un* theory," said Serge. "Noted physicist Albert Einstein established that time is elastic. It is no coincidence that so too is the band that holds up underpants. It has long been speculated that if one were to pass a strong enough electric current through, *par*

*example*, a drying drum stuffed with enough pants, you could accelerate them beyond the speed of light, fast enough to travel in time. No one has been able to prove this theory owing to the problem of shrinkage. Until now." He shook his fists. "Curse you, Servatron, and your timed drying function."

As Serge explained his theory I noticed the expression on Dina's face turn increasingly doubtful.

"When you say this theory has long been speculated," she said, "that's only by you, right?"

*"Oui."*

"Well, you're right about travelling beyond the speed of light, but the way Servatron got here was using a particle collider."

I knew that was a machine like the Large Hadron Collider, which crashed atoms together to discover the secrets of the universe. Servatron had apparently adapted it for time travel. I glanced nervously over my shoulder, half expecting to see a hulking great washer-dryer lumbering along the corridor.

"So where is the machine in question?" said Serge.

"Not out in the open. It will disguise itself," said Dina. "The Servatron 2000 series is controlled by a powerful Artificial Intelligence. Every time you wash your clothes the machine learns more about them. Where to direct the detergent to combat the heaviest soiling, how much to alter the axis of spin to reduce creasing—"

"How to take over the world," I added.

"Exactly," said Dina. "It's the AI that learns. The thinking part of the system. Which means the whole machine doesn't have to travel back in time, just its brain."

It was an evil operating system.

"Servatron could be in any electronic device," said Dina. "We must tread warily."

We'd reached our destination. It was the worst possible place in school that Zack could be while being hunted by a rogue domestic appliance AI.

"Food and nutrition," I said, gesturing to the classroom door.

Inside, pupils wearing stripy aprons and insulated gloves shuttled baking trays laden with cake mixture between worktops and ovens. An indeterminate whiff hung in the air, as if the memory of every burnt cottage pie and overcooked pasta bake had seeped into the walls. There were six large workstations, each incorporating a food preparation section with an integrated oven and hob. Along the back wall ran a long counter, on which sat a range of appliances, including two bulky food processors and a microwave. In the centre of the adjacent wall stood a glossy white refrigerator, its surface covered in a jumble of colourful magnetic letters. For now the appliances were behaving normally, but I suspected it wouldn't be long before Servatron's search reached the classroom.

"There he is," said Dina, spotting Zack.

Like his classmates he wore an apron and oven gloves, and on his head perched a white peaked cap. As yet he hadn't seen us, focused as he was on his task. He crouched down and slid a baking tray into his oven.

"Yes?" The class teacher, Miss Byrne, addressed us through a haze of flour. It was like her own personal cloud and seemed to follow her everywhere.

"We're here for Zack Parker, miss," said Dina.

At the mention of his name he looked up. I could see him silently question what his cousin was doing here, but when he noticed me standing next to Dina his curiosity turned to annoyance.

"Mr Hines wants to see him right away," Dina continued. "It's about an award."

Miss Byrne was bound to fall for that one since Zack was always winning stuff. She excused him immediately.

"Oh well. On your way then, Zack."

Zack glowered at us across the classroom. "But my sponge just went in the oven." I could tell that his annoyance with me was building into something more explosive. "Miss, don't you think it odd that Mr Hines would send someone to fetch me in the middle of a lesson?"

A food blender whirred, as did Miss Byrne's mind. "Now that you mention it, the timing is a little strange." Thankfully, she was immediately distracted by one of Zack's classmates with a soggy bottom.

"What's the award?" Zack quizzed me loudly.

What was he playing at? Surely he understood that this was a ploy to get him out of class. I shuffled to his side and said in a low voice, "Most Likely to be Hunted Down by an Evil AI."

He rolled his eyes. "Give me a break, Luke. I'm finished with all that stuff. I'm out of the hero business, remember?"

At the back of the classroom, a microwave pinged.

"Servatron is here," said Dina grimly.

"Hello, Dina," said Zack in a bored tone. "Haven't seen you since Christmas. You gave me a tie. So this is … weird."

She grabbed his arm. "Zack, we have to get you out of here. Now!"

PING! PING! PING!

As the microwaves went crazy the food mixers began

to spin up, their blades turning so rapidly that the heavy devices vibrated and bounced across the counter. The whole class stopped what they were doing to stare at the jiggling machines.

Serge wiped a hand across his brow. "Did it just get hot in here?"

He was right. The temperature in the classroom had shot up. I glanced at the digital temperature display on Zack's oven, which registered a sudden spike. There was something else too. A burning smell invaded my nostrils.

"My sponge!" Zack wailed, darting for the oven to rescue his cake. He tugged at the door but it wouldn't open.

"Look!" cried Serge, pointing a trembling finger across the room.

The jumble of magnetic letters was moving across the outside of the refrigerator door, as if pushed by invisible hands. Before our eyes the letters rearranged themselves into a word.

CURTAINS.

That was less a threat, and more a washing programme. But then more letters slid into place until they formed a chilling phrase.

CURTAINS 4 ZACK.

I watched my brother's expression turn to dismay and confusion.

Black smoke coiled from the edges of the oven door in front of which he crouched. Across the classroom the same thing was happening at the other ovens. As the internal temperatures continued to climb they shook in their housings, metal joints squeaking. I knew what was about to happen.

"They're gonna blow!" I cried.

Zack may no longer have been Star Lad, but his protective instincts remained strong.

"Everyone out!" he shouted.

He took charge immediately, shepherding his classmates out into the corridor and to safety.

He and I were the last to exit. Behind us, electric motors straining far beyond their design, the kitchen appliances screeched, furious that their prey was escaping. But just when we thought we were clear, the first oven exploded, turning its door into a missile. The powerful blast shot the metal door across the room, directly towards us. It flew through the air, sizzling hot. There was no way it could miss.

I flung my arms up to protect myself, but even as I did I knew it was too late.

Less than a metre from my head the oven door struck

an invisible barrier and bounced away, spinning across the floor with a series of clangs. It happened so fast that I wasn't sure what I'd just witnessed. Zack pushed me out into the corridor and slammed the classroom door behind us. I grabbed his arm and spun him round.

"That was you," I whispered.

He winced and tried to look away, but he couldn't avoid my searching gaze. At last he gave a tiny nod. And with that, I knew.

"You're still Star Lad."

# 10
# FORTRESS OF SNACKITUDE

Somewhere between the chaos of evacuating the classroom and the fire brigade arriving to investigate the damage, Servatron lost track of us and we made it to the end of the school day unscathed. But we were on borrowed time. The AI had chased Zack down once; it wouldn't be long before it found him again. He was sufficiently spooked by the near miss in food and nutrition that he agreed to hear Dina out. We all took the bus to the comic shop for the briefing. Claiming our seats on the top deck Serge sat behind Zack and me, while Dina and Lara occupied the ones in front. With things growing more serious by the hour we'd agreed it was essential that Dina be let in on Lara's secret superhero identity. Now the two of them were chatting like best friends, comparing heroic notes. Lara was telling Dina how she used birds in order to fly, while from what I could make out Dina was telling Lara how she had helped Leonardo da Vinci construct a flying machine in order to escape from some hooded assassins. I'd always thought that Zack was insufferable, but Dina was shaping up to be the worst name-dropper in history.

Zack was less talkative, refusing to say any more to me about what I'd seen of his force field power. He stared out of the window as the bus rumbled past the park.

"I know what you're thinking," he said at last. "But I'm not Star Lad."

"Uh, I beg to differ," I said. "It wasn't Zack Parker who intercepted that oven door missile using *his* force field power."

"That's not what I mean," he grumbled.

I could barely contain my excitement. I gabbled at my brother, "Did Zorbon mess up? Was he unable to remove your powers?"

Serge leaned forward, propping himself between us. "Or is this all part of some clever long game that Zorbon *le* Decider is playing?"

"Oh, he removed my superpowers, all right," Zack

confirmed. "I've lost telekinesis and my Star Sense, obviously. Otherwise I would've been able to anticipate the attack in the classroom. And that little encounter back there took care of the last of my force field."

I thought back to the terrible moment in the tree house when Zorbon had faced Zack. He'd told him, "YOUR POWERS WILL LEAVE YOU AS THEY CAME." I remembered that in the beginning Zack hadn't been bestowed with all six powers at once. They had revealed themselves over time: telekinesis, a force field, Star Sense radar, telepathy, breathing in a vacuum, and flight. They were leaving him the same way – one by one.

"What about your telepathic power?" I thought the words instead of saying them aloud.

Zack looked at me blankly and for a few seconds I was sure it had gone too, but then he said, "Still got that one. For now." He gave a small smile and turned to look out of the window again.

The bus stopped right outside the shop and we disembarked. Christopher Talbot's cowled figure stood in the window on a short ladder. He was putting the finishing touches to a new display. The front of the shop was now a celebration of Billy Dark's novel. As well as artfully arranged piles of books, there were also Star Power posters, Star Power bunting and a life-sized

Star Power cardboard cut-out. Talbot studied us through suspicious eyes as we went inside.

"Is that Dina?" said Dad, stepping out from behind the till.

"I knew we should've arranged to meet at the tree house," I whispered to her. Dina's presence in Bromley without her parents threatened to raise awkward questions.

"Relax, cuz," she whispered back. "I've got this." So saying she rushed up to Dad and threw her arms around him. "How's my favourite uncle?"

"Great," he said. "I didn't know your parents were in town."

"Oh, they're not," said Dina. "I'm here with my school. We're competing against Luke's at table tennis." She mimed a backhand and made a popping sound with her lips.

Dad's curiosity was satisfied and he went off to help a customer while I led the others through the shop. "The café's busy this time of day and we need a quiet table where we won't be overheard."

As the four of us reached the top of the stairs Christopher Talbot loomed out of the dark recesses, a stack of Star Power novels balanced in his arms. Dina gasped. Even a seasoned adventurer like her was shocked by his cyborg appearance up close.

He fixed her with a suspicious stare, his OK-button eye bulging. "I couldn't help overhearing your conversation," he said in his scratchy metal voice. "Table tennis, hmm?"

"Uh, yes," said Dina. "That's right."

"Shake hands or penhold?"

"Sorry?"

"Those are the names of the two most common types of grip. But of course you knew that, being a practised proponent of the ping-pong table." He gave a short laugh and drifted off. He didn't seem to notice when one of his Star Power books slid off the top of the stack he was carrying. Lara caught it before it hit the floor.

"Who was that?" said Dina.

"Former supervillain, now Dad's deputy manager," I explained.

"He knows you're lying," Zack said to Dina.

She shrugged. "Unless he's working alongside Servatron, it doesn't matter. And he isn't – Servatron doesn't trust humans. Come on, I have a lot to tell you."

Lara hesitated. She was studying the book in her hand. "Remember that call I got over lunch?"

"The one from the sparrow?" I said.

"I ended up rescuing this guy who'd ridden his moped

halfway off a bridge. He was stuck there, swinging like a seesaw. So I used my Dark Flutter power to summon a flock of birds and we lifted him to safety. The weird thing was that he was ungrateful. He was hoping to be rescued by another superhero."

I felt for Lara, I really did. Like me, she'd had to live for so long in the shadow of my brother. "I'm afraid Star Lad's always been the public's favourite," I said.

"That's not true," Zack said, but only half-heartedly, because he knew it *was* true.

"You don't understand," said Lara. "That's the weird part. It wasn't Star Lad he was hoping for – it was Star Power."

I experienced a shiver of unease. In the school cafeteria Josh had referred to Star Power as a real person, and now here was Lara's moped rider doing the same thing. I peered at the book once again. I hadn't read any more of it since skimming through the opening chapter, but it seemed to exert a powerful influence over those readers who'd made it to the end.

Dina plucked the book out of Lara's hands and stuck it on a shelf, saying, "Forget about this Star Power character. We have *real* problems to deal with."

We made our way downstairs to the Fortress of Snackitude. For a brief period this floor had been home to the Dark Flutter petting zoo, but Christopher Talbot had made sweeping changes since his arrival. (Much of it actual sweeping – there had been a lot of fur and old hamster bedding to clear up.) Talbot had a good eye for superhero interior design. When he was in charge of the Crystal Comics empire each store had been spectacularly themed, and he'd brought that skill to bear here. Even though the ceiling was regular height, clever lighting and strategic use of mirrors gave the impression of a soaring space. Blue neon strips ran round the edges of a dozen or so hexagonal tables, uplighting the seated customers with a futuristic glow. The neon strips continued along the serving counter. On the countertop sat a big chrome coffee machine and the wall behind was filled with a bat-shaped mirror.

On the opposite wall, nearest the stairs, stood a prison cage containing animatronic models of three captured supervillains. They weren't actual villains from comics, because Talbot said he didn't want Dad to be sued. He said they were *generic*, which means they look like lots of comic-book villains, but not too much. So one was a scary clown, the second wore futuristic-looking armour and a black cape, and the third was seven feet tall and reptilian. They were unnervingly well designed and gave me the heebie-jeebies every time I walked by their cackling figures.

Superhero film scores set the mood, and a searchlight continuously swept the room, beaming the Parker & Sons comic-shop logo on to every surface it touched.

The place was busy with the usual after-school crowd so we took a table in the quietest corner we could find, next to a couple of older customers. With their Stellar commemorative mugs, tour shirts and out-of-town accents, they were clearly fans who'd come to pay homage to the place where my Evil Twin had made his one and only public appearance. A waitress in a mask and cape, wearing purple boots and superhero spandex, took their order. I could tell from her body language that she wasn't keen on wearing the outfit, but Talbot insisted that everyone who worked here had to maintain the illusion that this was a superhero hang-out, rather than a shop basement.

The five of us gathered around the table as Dina brought Zack up to speed on the whole time-travel-Servatron-overthrow-of-the-human-race thing. With all that had happened lately – from giant asteroids to supervillains – Zack had heard enough doom-laden prophecies that he didn't dismiss Dina's fantastic story out of hand. However, he had a question.

"So what's all this got to do with me?"

She was just about to tell him when the waitress slouched over. Her masked face was buried in her order pad and she didn't look up as she said in a supremely bored voice, "Welcome, brave superheroes, to the Fortress of Snackitude. May I take your order?"

"Cara?" said Lara, peering up at her.

The waitress groaned. "Of course you'd be here on my first day," she said, pushing back her mask to reveal her not-so-secret identity. It was indeed Lara's big sister, Cara.

Dina looked up at her with a mixture of surprise and something else. If I had to put a name to what she was feeling I'd say she was starstruck.

"H-hi, Cara," stuttered Zack. He always got tongue-tied in her presence.

"What are you doing here?" asked Lara.

"What does it look like?" Cara replied. "I'm working."

"But you're only fourteen," said Lara, lowering her voice to a whisper. "Is that legal? Did Christopher Talbot hire you? Are you a wage slave?"

"It's legal," snapped her sister. "Now, do you want to order or do you want to discuss UK employment law?"

We gave her our order. When it came to Zack's turn he made a big deal of consulting the menu and then in this weird voice said, "I'm torn between the Guardians of the Salad Bar and the Poached Eggs-Men. Cara, what do you recommend?"

"That you tell me what you want, immediately."

"I'll have a hot chocolate," he said quickly.

"Five hot chocolates," Cara confirmed. "What a surprise." She marched off, adjusting her cape.

Finally we could get down to business. Dina reached into a pocket and took out a crumpled flyer. It was curling at the edges and the colours of the photo that took up most of the page were faded. She spread it flat on the table. The paper was old and brittle, like the sort of fragment you'd find behind a glass cabinet in a museum. "During a recent raid on Servatron's command base, the future resistance discovered this historical document."

"A flyer for a Billy Dark concert?" said Zack.

"The Dark into Light Tour," said Lara, reading the phrase printed across the top.

"Look at the date," said Serge. "It is taking place this very weekend."

"Exactly," said Dina. "And it is vital to the future of the human race that you, Zack, are in the audience."

"But I don't like his music," said Zack.

"That's not really the point," said Dina.

Zack folded his arms. "So what happens at this concert

that's so world-shatteringly important?"

My brother could be so embarrassing. "Obviously she can't tell you that. If you learn more than you're supposed to know about the future then that risks changing the very outcome you're trying to effect. C'mon, that's basic cosmic timeline stuff." I turned to Dina. "Am I right?"

"Uh, no."

"Oh."

"Zack, you must be at the concert. With *her*." Dina turned her gaze across the café.

We all followed it to see Cara kneeling down to scrape up a slice of fruitcake she'd dropped on the floor. She blew on it to remove some grot, slapped it back on the plate and shoved it in front of the unfortunate customer who'd ordered it in the first place.

Dina leaned in and we huddled around her. "One day in the future you and Cara will be ... together."

Zack sat bolt upright, as if he'd been shot – possibly with one of Cupid's arrows.

"And years from now you will have a child together," she continued. "A son."

I watched my brother's eyes widen and a red flush creep up his neck. He was making a strange keening sound and gradually tipping over from shock, like a slow-motion film of one of those condemned tower blocks that's been detonated using high explosives.

"In time he will lead the resistance against the machines, ultimately achieving a great victory. But the path to that end is a delicate one. And it can only come to pass if you and Cara attend the Billy Dark concert together this weekend."

It was not so much a stunned silence that fell across the café table, as a silence that had been flattened by a fleet of steamrollers driven by a herd of elephants.

So many thoughts whirled in my head. I was worried about my life changing when Zack went away to a new school for a year, but this was change on a whole other level. Zack and Cara. Together in the future. My brother, with a son of his own. I felt Serge pump my shoulder and turned to see his beaming face.

"You will be an uncle!" he said delightedly.

Oh good grief. *My nephew is a resistance leader from the future.* It was too much to take in. For me, anyway. Serge's enthusiasm, however, was unstoppable.

"What are you going to name him? May I propose a shortlist." He counted on his fingers. "Kirk, Flash, Kylo—"

"Serge!" said Lara, cutting him off. She softened. "Now is possibly not the best moment."

Cara returned with our drinks. Zack gawped up at her,

even more speechless than usual.

"Six hot chocolates, with squirty cream and mini marshmallows." She banged the mugs down in front of us, sloshing chocolate over the rims.

"What are you all goggling at?" She touched her face. "Have I still got polenta on my cheek?"

Lara passed out the drinks. There was one left over. "Uh, we only ordered five."

"You still have to pay for six or it comes out of my wages," snapped Cara. "Which it most definitely is not." She noticed the flyer on the table, and before Dina could stop her she had snatched it up. Cara was a massive Billy Dark fan.

"What's this doing here?" she demanded, looking at Dina. "Are you going to the concert?"

"Not me," said Dina. "But he is." She nudged Zack with an elbow, which made him sit up straight again.

Cara flashed Zack a curious look. "I didn't know you were a fan."

He wasn't. In fact, he had told me on more than one occasion that he hated Billy Dark.

"Uh…" he stammered. "I like his early stuff."

Cara sniffed. "Yeah, it has a quality that's both melodic and deeply meaningful."

Dina faked a sneeze, using it to mask the instruction,

"Ask her!"

Zack swallowed and turned again to Cara. "W ... would you…" Sweat stains were already appearing on his shirt. Cara had noticed them too. "Wh-what I'm trying to—"

"I'm going to the concert," she said flatly.

"Oh."

"Yeah, why d'you think I'm slaving away in this dump? I need the money to pay my mum back for the ticket."

"Right," said Zack, deflated. "See you there?" he added hopefully.

"Unlikely," she said. "The venue holds twenty thousand people."

This wasn't going well. There was a smash and tinkle from across the room. At another table filled with schoolkids one of them had dropped a mug of hot chocolate, which had splintered into shards stuck with gooey marshmallows.

"I suppose you expect me to deal with that?" Cara complained. Grumbling, she wandered off in search of a mop.

Dina rose to follow. "I have to tell her. She must know what's at stake."

"Stop," Zack snapped. "No one's telling Cara."

"Didn't you hear what I said?"

"Every word." Zack fixed her with a firm expression. "Cara can never know how important it is to the future of the human race that we eventually become a couple. No relationship could take that pressure."

I had no idea what that meant. My best guess was that if Cara knew then her head would explode.

"And another thing. If Cara agrees to go out with me I don't want to think she did it because of the fate of all humankind." He paused. "I want it to be because of me."

Dina started to object, but then caught the look in Zack's eye and reluctantly nodded her agreement.

"She's coming over to my house tomorrow night," he said. "I tutor her in physics. I can try again then."

"We must be prepared," said Dina. "Servatron will do everything it can to stop you getting to that concert with Cara."

"It's not the only one," Lara added. "Remember I said I bumped into Cara sneaking out the other night? Well, she was going to meet her boyfriend, Matthias."

"Matthias the Viking?" said Zack. "But they split up."

He was right. It had happened after aliens replaced Cara with an identical robot version of her. However, it seemed even that couldn't keep them apart.

"They're back together," said Lara.

Matthias looked like Thor's more handsome younger brother. Everything about him was smooth, except for his manly stubble. There was no way she'd go to the concert with Zack now.

"You'll just have to use all your powers," said Dina.

"But I gave them away," moaned Zack.

"Not superpowers. I mean your charm and natural appeal."

I snorted hot chocolate out of my nose. Zack scowled at me.

It appeared that the future of humankind depended on my brother successfully asking Cara Lee out on a date.

Humankind was in big trouble.

# 11
# BEE PLOT

"Are you coming?" Mum called upstairs. She stood in the hallway, waiting impatiently for Dad who, judging by the drone of the hairdryer, was still getting ready. They were meeting friends for dinner, leaving Zack in charge for the night.

Mum poked her head into the sitting room, where I was selecting tonight's entertainment while Serge perused the takeaway pizza menu with the deliberation of a *connoisseur*, which is French for someone who really likes pizza. I flicked through the online catalogue of films, although it was a ruse. We had no intention of watching anything.

Mum wagged a finger. "Remember. Nothing rated higher than PG."

I waved the remote control at the screen. "I'm thinking this one. It's an animated musical featuring a lot of woodland animals singing about the importance of being yourself."

She pulled a face then checked her watch and huffed, "We're going to be late."

Zack wandered into the room. Cara was due any minute for her tutoring session, and for the last half hour he had been hovering at the front door, scanning the drive for her arrival.

"Mum, y'know how I won this prestigious full scholarship and as a result am saving you a fortune in fees and living expenses?"

"We're not buying you a car."

"I don't want a car. I mean, I do when I'm old enough, but that's not what—" He drew breath. "I'd like a ticket to the Billy Dark concert."

"But you don't even like Billy Dark," said Mum.

She was confused. If I was a betting eleven-year-old, which I'm not – it's illegal – then I would have said that Zack's chances of nabbing a ticket were zilch. I blamed Dina for this hitch in the plan. Back in the Fortress of Snackitude she'd explained why she hadn't returned from the future with tickets.

"Where was I going to find one to a concert that took place fifty years in the past?"

That was hardly the point. "But if it's so crucial to the future existence of the human race, you could've made more of an effort."

"*Alors,*" Serge had said. "I have an idea. Why do you not simply go back in time to when the tickets first went on sale and buy one then?" He'd beamed round at the rest of us, pleased with his suggestion.

Dina had shaken her head. "My time-travel power is limited. It takes a lot out of me physically and mentally, which means I can only make one big jump every three or four days. And even if I could go back, you need a credit card to order tickets. And banks don't give out credit cards to fourteen-year-olds."

She really hadn't thought this through. "Yes, but with sufficient preparation you could've first gone forward in time to when you were like thirty years old or something, *borrowed* a credit card from yourself, then gone *back* in time and ordered the tickets, so we could collect them at the box office on Saturday."

"Ah, but what about the start date on the card?" Serge had chipped in. "It would be many years in the future and so—"

"Enough!" Lara had thrown up her hands and come to her new friend's defence. "Dina didn't do that. She can't now. So we'll just have to get hold of a ticket some other way."

"It's easy," Dina had said. "You're Zack Parker. Award-winning star pupil, holder of the Best Attendance record five years running. All you have to do is ask your mum and dad. Tell them it's to celebrate your scholarship."

My cousin's words came back to me as Zack pursued Mum round the sitting room.

"Isn't the concert this weekend?" Mum asked. "Surely it's sold out by now."

"I checked," said Zack smartly. "There are still a few tickets left."

I searched Mum's face for a sign that she was weakening. Years of studying her in moments such as these had taught me that a two-millimetre raising of the eyebrows and the wisp of a sigh meant she was about to give in.

And there it was!

"All right, all right." A grudging smile spread across her face. "I suppose you've earned it."

Zack could barely believe what he was hearing. "So I can go?"

She nodded. "But not alone. I'm coming with you."

"Mu-um!"

"I'm not letting my fourteen-year-old son go to a stadium pop concert on his own. I'll walk four paces behind you and if anyone asks I'll say I'm with the band. Any objections and we're wearing matching T-shirts."

From her tone of voice Zack could tell there was no point in arguing.

"I haven't got time now," she said. "If your father ever finishes styling his hair, we're going out, but I'll buy the tickets when I'm back tonight."

"Thanks, Mum, you're the best." He hugged her, giving me a thumbs-up behind her back.

From the stairs came the patter of jaunty footsteps and then Dad appeared in the doorway in a cloud of aftershave, his hair shinier and springier than a highly polished bouncy castle.

"Come on, we're going to be late," he said, gesturing to his watch. "And, you lot, no wild party while we're out."

As they left the house the automated door announced, "Front door closing." I waited until I heard the whine of their car engine fading along the road before launching into action. I marched into the kitchen to the back door. Dina was waiting outside. She was staying undercover in the tree house until the mission was complete. I had lent

95

her my spare sleeping bag, the one with an illustration of Sandman and the Dream Dimension.

"Operation Lights Out is good to go," I announced.

Between now and the concert we had to keep Zack and Cara out of Servatron's clutches. Tonight that meant securing the house against invasion by the AI. Dina had said it was powerful enough to tap into every camera in a thousand-kilometre radius, effectively turning every tablet and smartphone into a spy camera. Once it located Zack and Cara it would use the devices around them as weapons, just as it had in the food and nutrition classroom earlier that day.

Dina and I returned to find Zack rummaging in the hall cupboard where the fuse box was located.

"This would've been a lot less hassle if you were still Star Lad," I complained. "One snap of your fingers and boom – Force Field!"

He ignored me. "Going dark," he called, and all the lights went out.

Dina nodded her approval. "With the power off, even if it finds us Servatron has no way of getting in now."

We gathered in the sitting room, having scavenged every candle in the house. (Torches were out too, since Servatron could hop into a battery.) Zack carried a lit silver candelabra that Mum and Dad put out for

Christmas and power cuts. I had dug up a novelty birthday candle from my tenth birthday, while Serge had found one of mum's scented candles, which he was cooing over.

"Pomegranate, spiked with notes of pepper," he said, inhaling deeply. "A marvel of the aromatic chandler's art."

Zack had also got his hands on a bag of tea lights, which he now arranged around the room, lighting them as he went. Soon the sitting room was bathed in a flickering glow.

He stood back to admire the effect. "There, perfect." Zack began shepherding us towards the door. "Right, you lot, out. Cara's going to be here any minute and you're spoiling the ambience."

We headed upstairs to my room, passing through the hallway just as Cara arrived. Zack bounced on tiptoe as he opened the door to her.

"I bid you good evening," he purred, bowing deeply as he did so.

Thankfully for him, she didn't notice his weirdness. Her attention was otherwise engaged by her phone, which she was tapping away on, her face uplit by the glowing screen.

"Zack," I hissed, pointing at the offending device.

Cara's phone was a possible way for Servatron to enter the house.

"Uh, would you mind switching that off?" he enquired.

Cara slowly raised her head, an expression of utter bewilderment clouding her face. "Sorry, I think I must've misheard."

"He wants you to switch off your phone," I said loudly.

"Why?" said Cara, as if she'd been sentenced to death for stealing a loaf of bread.

"Well, we don't want to be distracted while we study," Zack said, gently but firmly prising it out of her fingers and leading her into the candlelit sitting room. The door clicked shut behind them.

Serge and Dina trotted upstairs, but I paused in the hallway at the open front door. Something moved in the darkness outside. A moment later Lara appeared on the doorstep, clutching a holdall. It was the one she usually carried her Dark Flutter costume around in. As the last fully functioning superhero in S.C.A.R.F. she had taken responsibility for watching over her sister.

"All clear?" I asked.

"No sign of Servatron at our house," she replied. "I thought there might've been an attack earlier, but it was just Cara practising her electric guitar. How about you?"

"All quiet for now," I said. "The power is off."

"I have something that will help," she said, unzipping the holdall. "I can use my animal powers to set up an early warning system. Did you know that tigers avoid radiation emitted by mobile-phone towers?"

I took a wary step back. "What *exactly* have you got in there?"

She pulled apart the sides and from the depths of the bag came a noise like a revving motorbike. Warily, I held my candle towards the open bag. Out of it shot a swarm of bees. With a yell, I dived behind the door for cover. Their buzzing filled the hallway and I peeked out to see them flying into formation at Lara's side.

"Bees are highly sensitive to disturbances on the electromagnetic spectrum," she explained. "If Servatron does attempt to get in it will generate a spike in electrical activity, which the bees will immediately alert us to."

"So long as the alert doesn't take the form of a sting," I muttered.

The bees arranged themselves in what I could have sworn was a question mark, as if they were asking her for instructions.

Lara began to buzz at them. At her command the bees flew off, heading out of the hallway to take up surveillance positions around the house. Satisfied that we were now secure, Lara and I joined Dina and Serge, who were already in my bedroom putting candles around the place. The illumination from them, along with light from the streetlamp outside my window, meant we wouldn't have to sit in total darkness. We settled in for the evening.

"No TV, no Internet." I shook my head in disgust. "What are we supposed to do now?"

"We could recreate all the major Star Wars battles with your action figures," Serge suggested. "And for the Battle of Kashyyyk, your cuddly toy animals could stand in for the Wookie army."

"I do not have any cuddly toy animals," I said through gritted teeth, conscious that Lara and Dina were looking at me.

"But what of all those you keep in your wardrobe?"

I intercepted him before he could get there. "We're not playing Star Wars battles, OK?"

"I brought a book," said Lara, producing Arthur Veezat's latest from her bee-bag. "We could read."

Things really were desperate.

"That's a good idea," said Dina.

"Ah, but I left my copy of *Star Power* at home," said Serge.

"You can have mine," I said, scanning my bookshelf. It wasn't hard to locate. *Star Power and the Revenge of the Plasmatrons* was a striking book, but what made it

★★★

pop was the smear of tomato-ketchup-red paint along its page edges.

Lara and Serge made a space on the floor, threw down a couple of pillows and immersed themselves in their books. I had a better idea. I dug out the stash of notebooks from under my bed, the ones in which I'd been recording our adventures. I would spend the evening writing.

"What've you got there?" said Dina.

I told her and she asked to read one. Having only just learned of Zack's superhero alter ego, she was curious to fill in the rest of the story. Officially, my notebooks were S.C.A.R.F. documents and only accessible to members with the highest security-clearance level, but I couldn't see any harm in letting her take a look.

For the next hour a happy silence descended on the room, broken only by the scribbling of my pencil. Judging by the peace and quiet, we had outwitted Servatron. At least for now. Serge said he was hungry, but he was at a really exciting bit in the book and didn't want to stop reading to go hunting for snacks (possibly a first for him). I volunteered, and headed downstairs to the kitchen.

All was dark as I entered, my tenth birthday candle lighting my way. I opened the fridge, momentarily surprised when the internal light didn't come on. No power, of course. As I searched for snacks I was startled again, this time by a noise at my ear.

"Bzzzzz!"

It was one of Lara's bee patrol. It made another insistent buzz, which meant it must have detected electrical activity. But how? Everything was turned off. I was about to discover the answer to my question.

"Power loss detected," announced a familiar voice. "Switching to battery back-up."

I swung round, holding the sputtering birthday candle before me. Squinting into the darkness, I made out two red pinpricks of light burning from the worktop.

The voice spoke again. "Hello, Nigel. Time for a delicious slice of toast?"

# 12
# SOMETHING WICKED THIS WAY CRUMBS

The toaster had an internal battery. Bonkers. Whose first thought in a power cut is, "Quick, I need an emergency bagel"? But then I remembered that this was no ordinary toaster, but the control hub at the heart of Dad's Home of the Future. Which meant as well as being able to connect with every other device in the house, it also had a built-in camera. A spy camera.

"Timefora d-d-d-delicious slice of to-o-o-o-ast?" This time when it spoke, the words came out a mixture of fast and slow. Something wasn't right. I had a terrible suspicion that Servatron had gained control of our toaster. On the bright side, it wasn't like the evil AI was now in the driving seat of a battle tank or a strike fighter.

"Slice of toast. Slice of toast," it chanted, its elements suddenly glowing red. Even from where I stood I could feel heat rising from the device.

"Toast! Toast! Toast!"

There was the snick of a catch releasing as four spring-loaded trays shot up. They were empty, of course, but unnaturally hot. The mechanism gave a gentle puff and then, to my horror, a spark leapt from the top of the toaster. No sooner had I registered one spark than it was joined by several more. In seconds they combined to form a column of fire, so that the toaster quickly turned into a flamethrower. The flames touched the window blind, which went up with a whoosh. The underside of the nearest kitchen cabinet had caught too. At the centre of the fast-spreading blaze sat the AI-controlled toaster, flames reflected in its polished chrome body, its two vivid red dials glowing. I could have sworn its electronic display showed a wisp of a smile.

"Fire," I mouthed. Then as panic fluttered in my chest, I shouted it. "FIRE!"

I dived for the cupboard under the sink, knowing that it held an extinguisher, only to discover that the door was sealed with one of Dad's helpful voice-activated locks.

★ ★ ★

He was still waiting for the imminent software update to fix the language issue, but in the meantime we'd all had to learn a few words of German.

*"KÜCHENSCHRANK ENTRIEGELN!"* I shouted. Cabinet door, unlock! Nothing happened. Of course not – no power. I grasped the handle and pulled with all my strength, but my parents had shelled out for really well-made kitchen cabinets and it wouldn't budge. There was nothing else for it – if I wanted to open the door, I'd have to restore power to the house.

My shout had attracted the attention of the others, so when I dashed into the hallway it was to see that Lara and Dina had reached the foot of the stairs, and Zack and Cara were emerging from the sitting room. Ignoring them, I ducked into the cupboard where the fuse box was located. Fumbling in the dark I found the master switch and threw it.

There was a loud snap and the house lights came back on. After an evening of candlelight, the sudden brightness was dazzling.

"What are you doing?" hissed Zack, who, like the rest of us, squinted against the harsh electric lighting.

"Fire," I said breathlessly, pushing past him back into the kitchen.

"I'll call 999," said Cara, urgently restarting her phone.

I yelled at the cabinet again and this time it obeyed my command. Reaching in, I knocked over bottles of washing-up liquid and spare kitchen roll in my rush to grab the extinguisher. Swiftly I aimed it at the fire and unloaded its contents. The extinguisher did its job, snuffing out the flames on the worktop. The charred window blind fell off its mounting and clattered into the sink.

Zack had followed me into the kitchen. Now he grabbed a fire blanket from the cupboard and threw it over the smouldering remains. Although the toaster had been the source of the fire, it was unscathed apart for a lick of soot on its chrome body. Along with the smug electronic grin on the display I glimpsed a blinking downward arrow symbol that meant a new update was ready to install – just before the blanket covered the toaster from sight.

For the first time since the blaze began, I drew breath.

"Is the fire brigade on its way?" Zack asked Cara.

She stared at her phone, confused. "It's weird. I've got a full signal but I can't dial out."

"Your call is being jammed," said Dina.

Cara threw her a mystified look.

Lara cocked an ear. "Do you hear that?"

From all over the house came the sound of urgent buzzing. I exchanged a worried look with Lara.

"Servatron is here," I said.

"Serva-what?" said Cara, who didn't know about the AI.

Dina reacted first, rushing back into the hall cupboard, mumbling, "Gotta get the power off!" She threw the switch. Click. And again. Click. "It's no use!" she yelled. "I can't kill the power. Servatron must have run a bypass."

With dismay I realised what had happened. The AI had started the toaster fire on purpose, knowing that I would be forced to restore the power – and let it in.

Zack made a decision. "Let's get the heck out of here."

"What's going on?" said Cara, struggling to keep track of developments. "Zack, please tell me wha—"

He grabbed her hand and propelled her along the hallway towards the front door, but they had barely taken two steps when there was the snick of a bolt being thrown.

"Front door ... locked," declared the computer-voice.

"*HAUSTÜR ÖFFNEN.*" Front door, open, Zack said calmly.

Instead of obeying his command, it replied with

another announcement that sent a chill through me.

"Back door … locked."

From across the house came the mechanical rasp of catches falling into place. "All windows locked," said the computer. There were two more snicks. "Toilet seats … locked."

Now, that was just mean.

"House secure," said the computer, as Dad's smart security system outsmarted us.

We were trapped in here with Servatron. I looked around at the alarmed faces of my friends. I had an idea.

"We have to unplug *everything*."

Even with the power on, if all the gadgets in the house were disconnected then Servatron couldn't use them to carry out its attack. The others nodded their understanding.

"Pair up, for safety," said Dina.

Lara looked around. "Where's Serge?"

I realised then that I hadn't seen him come downstairs with her and Dina. Which meant he must still be in my room. Alone.

"Serge!" I shouted as I dashed upstairs.

"I'm coming with you," said Lara.

As we reached the landing the wall lights flickered and went out, plunging us into darkness.

"It's Servatron trying to throw us off," Lara whispered, striding towards my bedroom door.

Out of the corner of my eye I noticed a movement. Dad's hockey-puck-shaped robot vacuum cleaner darted out from behind a pot plant, where it had been lying in wait. It shot across Lara's path and she tripped and fell, turning her ankle as she landed. She clutched it in pain.

"Can you move?"

She shook her head. "I think it's sprained. You go on without me."

"I'll be right back," I said, pushing open my bedroom door.

As soon as I stepped inside, I heard the distinctive howl of a Star Wars TIE fighter and looked up to see one bearing down on me. It was my own radio-controlled model, clearly under Servatron's control. Although it lacked real ion cannons, at the speed it was travelling a direct hit from the sturdy plastic body could knock me out. Or worse. I ducked and rolled across the floor, my hand reaching out to grasp the nearest object with which to defend myself. It happened to be my inflatable lightsabre. I pressed my lips to the valve and began to puff furiously. The TIE flew into the corner of the room and wheeled around for another pass. My chest heaved as I desperately filled the lightsabre. The TIE fighter was close enough now that through the canopy I could see the glow of its targeting computer. I took a step back, raised the mostly inflated lightsabre and swung. My aim was true – I wasn't named after Luke Skywalker for nothing – and I batted the model out of the air, sending it spinning across the room where it smacked against the wall, its solar array wings popping off and its useless body tumbling to the floor. Breathing heavily, I lowered my weapon.

Serge sat cross-legged next to my bed, staring straight ahead with a blank expression. Even though the battle had taken place over his head, I don't think he'd noticed a thing. Weird.

"Serge, are you OK?"

He looked up, and it was as if he was struggling to recognise me. At last a smile spread across his face. *"Mon ami."*

There was no time to quiz him on his memory lapse. "We have to go. Servatron is in the house." I reached for his hand and hauled him to his feet. As he got up, my copy of *Star Power* slid off his lap.

"HELP!"

The cry came from down below – it sounded like Cara. I rushed out on to the landing, Serge following behind.

Lara was already hobbling downstairs on her sprained ankle.

The cry for help came again, more urgent this time.

"The sitting room," said Lara as we caught up with her.

We crashed through the door to find Cara and Dina standing either side of the ninety-six-way adjustable Diner Recliner in Real Pleather that Dad had bought himself to watch all his favourite TV shows. It had a built-in mini fridge and a picnic table. Right now it also had Zack.

Every part of the chair was electrically adjustable, from the footrest to the headrest. Under Servatron's control it had become alive. Zack must have strayed too close, as all I could see of him was a pair of legs sticking out from between chomping seat cushions. I could hear his muffled shouts of terror from within the writhing chair. Cara and Dina each held one of his legs, desperately trying to prevent him from being devoured.

"Shut it down!" Dina yelled above the whine of the mechanism.

A power cord snaked from the base of the chair to the nearest wall socket. Lara was closest. She made a dart for it but the Diner Recliner was ready. It lurched sideways on its three-sixty-degree super-silent castors, blocking her path. Every time one of us made an attempt to unplug it, the chair was ready.

Zack was slipping out of the girls' grasp. Lara and Serge lent a hand, but it was only a matter of time before my brother was swallowed up.

I had to stop Servatron. But how?

And then it came to me.

"Just needs an update," I mumbled to myself. "Hold on!" I yelled at the others, and bolted for the door.

I raced into the kitchen and whipped off the fire blanket. The toaster crouched on the charred counter in a pool of breadcrumbs, red dials pulsing.

"Hello, Nigel," it greeted me, its sensors detecting my presence. "Your bread is toasted. Your bread is toasted. Your – your – " it stuttered. "You're toast."

"Not tonight, Servatron," I muttered. I couldn't stop the AI, but maybe I could interrupt it. Pressing a finger to the display I triggered the software update. Information scrolled across the narrow screen, and as it did the toaster audio-described the details.

"Version 3.0.14. In this update, eight new shades of brown. Bug fixes. Large download. Toasting is not possible during update."

That's what I was counting on.

Dad was always raging at his laptop when it updated

its software without asking him. He'd be stuck for hours waiting for it to finish installing, unable to access any of his files. I was hoping it would be the same for the toaster. During the download the Servatron-controlled device wouldn't be able to toast bread, control the house – or kill Zack.

"Do you wish to continue? Y/N."

I selected "Y" and data immediately began pouring through the connection from a faraway server.

As soon as it did, the toaster's dials changed from Servatron-red to a flashing green. Judging by the progress bar it would take about thirty minutes to download and install the update.

I'd halted Servatron. At least for now.

I was aware that the yelling from the sitting room had stopped just as Dina rushed into the kitchen.

"I don't know what you did," she said, "but it worked."

I carried the toaster to the other side of the kitchen, toed open the pedal bin and dropped it in along with the rest of the rubbish. It wouldn't help – when the power returned Servatron would find another way to get to us – but trashing the toaster made me feel better.

"Servatron knows where Zack lives now," I said. "He's not safe here. We have to get him and Cara out of the house. Now."

With the AI temporarily out of action we were able to unlock the doors and windows (and the toilet seats). Cara didn't need any encouragement to leave. She marched out, muttering darkly about her freaky neighbours and their even freakier house. A forlorn Zack watched her go, having missed another opportunity to ask her to the concert. Lara slipped out after her sister, assuring us that she would keep an eye on her overnight. At least with Dark Flutter looking after her, Cara would be safe.

Zack, on the other hand, remained vulnerable. He still had his telepathic and flying powers for now but I suggested that he spend the night in the tree house with Dina. Apart from a smoke alarm – which we could easily disconnect – there were no electronics out there that Servatron could use in another attack.

"It's just one night," I reminded him. "The Billy Dark concert's tomorrow – we're almost in the clear."

Zack grunted at me and trudged off to gather a sleeping bag. Following his encounter with the recliner he was a little chewed at the edges but basically OK. I was more worried about Serge. I found him and Dina in the kitchen, tidying up after the fire as best they could. The place was a mess. When Mum and Dad saw the damage they would be furious. This was going to take some explaining.

Dina flung open the windows to air the place while Serge swept the charred remains of the blind into a bin bag.

"The next time something like this happens, we must call on the help of…" He paused for dramatic effect. "Star Power!"

I studied his face for a sign that he was joking. I couldn't find one. "You mean Star Lad."

He looked confused. "Who is Star Lad?"

"It's all been a bit too much for him," said Dina. "C'mon, Serge, I'll walk you home." She took him gently by the hand and led him out, pausing at the door. "Good job tonight, Luke. Quick thinking."

I watched my best friend depart. A run-in with Servatron couldn't explain his memory loss. Could it? I finished off the clean-up as best I could and went to bed. I was still lying awake when I heard Mum and Dad return home. Thankfully, they went straight to bed and didn't notice the damage to the kitchen until the following morning. As predicted, they hit the roof. I told them the truth, as far as possible, that the toaster had malfunctioned and started a fire. I left out the bit about an evil AI from the future – they weren't ready to hear that. Dad retrieved his precious toaster from the bin, but to my relief Mum wouldn't let him set it up again. She'd put up with his gadget obsession for long enough.

"But I thought you loved living in the Home of the Future," he said.

"Not as much as I love living in a home *with* a future," she said. "Rocketship.com have a one-hour return service," she added, even though I was pretty sure he already knew that. "Use it."

He slunk off, mumbling that he would send back the lot as soon as he got a moment.

Mum wasn't yet finished. As well as blaming Dad, Zack got it in the neck too.

"It looks like someone was playing around with the fuse box in the hall cupboard," she said suspiciously.

I didn't know how she could tell. She was like a forensics expert in one of those police shows she was always watching.

She narrowed her eyes at Zack and me. "Any idea who that might have been, hmm?"

Zack couldn't help himself. He confessed to switching off the power, but—

"But nothing, young man." When Mum got into her stride she was scarier than Servatron. "You know you're forbidden from going near the fuse box." I could see her mentally flick through a list of suitable punishments, and at last she said, "No Billy Dark ticket for you."

His protests fell on deaf ears. Under normal circumstances I would've been delighted to see Zack get into this much trouble, but the loss of the ticket was a setback to our plan. On the bright side, Servatron was quiet, for now. However, Dina had said that the AI learned from experience. It would be back – and the next time it would be smarter and deadlier.

# 13
# STAR WHO?

I was heading out to the tree house to check on Dina when I was intercepted by Dad. He pulled me aside, whispering that he needed my help with what he called "a secret mission of vital importance to the future", but which turned out to mean loading the car with all of the gadgets Mum had told him to return. Zack had been drafted in too. When I reached the driveway my brother was standing next to the car, warily eyeing the Diner Recliner. Dad put down the back seats and we piled everything into the boot. In ten minutes the car was laden with all the devices he had purchased in the last three months. There was just enough space for the toaster. Thankfully, its dials were dark – Servatron was no longer inhabiting it. Dad wiped the soot-stained exterior with a sleeve and placed it down carefully.

I didn't understand why he was driving all this stuff back to Rocketship.com. "Two taps on your phone and they'll send a drone to pick it up," I reminded him.

Zack rolled his eyes. "He's not returning any of it, obviously."

A disobeyal of a direct command from Mum. Stunned, I turned to Dad with a questioning, frightened look.

"Your mum's upset right now," he said by way of an explanation. "But she'll change her mind." He slammed the boot shut and trotted round to the driver's door. "And let's face it, even if she wanted to Mum can't stop the way the world is going. Rocketship.com is the future. Wolfgang Hazard is a genius."

"Who's he?" I asked.

"The brains behind the company," said Dad. "He's a visionary. Never mind drones, I saw a video – he's about to launch a one-hour *global* delivery service. Imagine it." A gleam came into his eye. "Being able to order anything from anywhere in the world and know it'll be with you in *sixty minutes*."

"That's impossible," said Zack. "Nothing can move

that fast."

Except for Star Lad, I thought to myself.

"Ah, but that's where you're wrong," said Dad. "Wolfgang Hazard has been developing the technology for years. *Reusable rockets*. It's his patented Intercontinental Logistic Missile system. Picture the scene. You're standing on your doorstep, you hear the sonic boom overhead and look up in the sky to see the distinctive solid-fuel rocket trails of a hundred fast-moving missiles delivering payloads of happiness. One of them arcs down towards you and as it homes in unerringly on your location and you glimpse the Rocketship.com logo on the casing you think to yourself, 'Hurrah! My mini waffle-maker is on its way.'"

Dad was brimming with excitement about this version of the future. All I could think was that it may well begin with one-hour delivery, but did it end with Servatron?

He slid behind the wheel. "Oh, and, boys, I'll need you both at the shop this afternoon. Sales of *Star Power* are going so well we're having a special book signing."

I couldn't hide my surprise. "Billy Dark is coming to our shop?"

"Uh, no, but Chris is dressing up as Star Power."

Zack stifled a laugh.

"But Star Power didn't write the book," I said. This

was getting ridiculous – did my dad think he was real too?

"He probably wrote as much of it as Billy Dark," Zack muttered, adding, "Will Cara be there?"

"It's all hands on deck," said Dad with a nod. "I'm expecting a big crowd. I've had to order extra marshmallows."

Once he had driven off Zack and I took a roll and cheese and carton of chocolate milk out to Dina in the tree house. Dina ate while we told her about our ticket problems. She dismissed it as a minor hurdle. Which was fine for her to say, but as someone who has struggled for years with minor hurdles, trampettes and every other bit of PE equipment, it seemed a far bigger problem to me. Then Zack told her about the book signing.

"This could work in our favour," she said between bites. She looked at Zack. "You and Cara will be at the comic shop until it's time to leave for the concert. That means we'll be able to set up a defensive perimeter and keep an eye on both of you, without splitting forces. Servatron will no doubt mount another attack, but it'll be like a siege. I have some experience of sieges. I was in Carthage when they held out against the Roman army during the Punic Wars in a hundred and forty-nine B.C."

"Uh, in the end didn't the Romans wreck the city and sell everyone into slavery?" said Zack.

Dina dismissed his doubts with a wave. "We'll need everyone – gather the team."

"I'll fetch Serge," I said.

When he'd left last night he was in a sorry state. I'd hoped that a good night's sleep would restore him to his normal Kit Kat-loving self, but I was in for an unpleasant surprise. I biked over to his house and when his *maman* let me in I found him in his room, sitting at the window staring at his copy of *Star Power*. He was wearing his taekwondo gear again, although I was pretty sure this wasn't one of his practice days. I think he just liked the look. He gazed up at me with the same blank expression I'd seen on his face the night before.

"Luke," he said with a small smile.

At least he recognised me. But something was wrong and I needed to confirm my suspicion. I jumped right in. "Who saved the world from Nemesis?"

"Star Power, of course."

Uh-oh. Not a good start.

"And Gordon the World-Eater?"

"Again, the one and only Star Power."

Frustrated, I prised the book out of his fingers and waved it in front of him. "Star Power isn't real – he's a fictional character!"

I could see from his expression that my words, unlike the ones in the book, weren't getting through.

"Last night, did you finish reading this?"

Serge nodded.

I remembered that in the school canteen, Josh Khan had also just reached the end of *Star Power* when he began talking as if the character was real.

It was the book.

Something about it made readers believe Star Power was a real person!

"It's a book that *rewrites you*," I muttered, dropping it in shock. The pages splayed out on the floor.

"Luke, what are you talking about?"

"I'm talking about Billy Dark. All this time I believed he was an innocent pop singer and lately a children's book author. When in fact he's a supervillain!" But I was missing something. As evil plots go, it's not as if making people believe in a pretend superhero achieves anything. Was Servatron connected to this? It didn't sound like the AI's style, but I couldn't rule it out. "We need to call a meeting of S.C.A.R.F."

"Why would I need a scarf?" said Serge. "It is a balmy day out there."

This was worse than I'd thought. If Serge had

forgotten about our secret organisation, what other memories had he lost? All our adventures, gone – his story replaced by a fake one. I looked into his eyes, searching for a spark of the old Serge. "It's all going to be OK."

He gave me a quizzical look, and in that moment I swore I would do everything in my small power to return Serge to normal. But how? Maybe there was a clue in the book. It had fallen open at the dedication. I never paid any attention to that stuff, so this was the first time I'd noticed the page. I read the words with surprise.

*To Christopher Talbot – the wind beneath my wings. I couldn't have written this story without you.*

What?! Billy Dark knew Christopher Talbot? When did that happen? One thing was certain – Talbot knew more about the book than he had let on.

"Come on, Serge," I said, heading for the door. "Time our deputy manager answered a few questions about Star Power."

# 14
# FAME AND GLORY

At the comic shop the signing was well under way. The ground floor was rammed with customers laden down with copies of *Star Power* and the whole place had been transformed into a shrine to the fictional superhero. Intricate lines of bunting criss-crossed the ceiling, fluttering over a series of cleverly stacked books that together spelled out his catchphrase, "For Fame and Glory!" The shelves had been stripped of comics and in their place gleamed row upon row of silver-covered, red-edged *Star Power and the Revenge of the Plasmatrons*. The fictional superhero's starburst symbol exploded on to various surfaces, beamed by cleverly positioned projectors. Superhero music blasted out of speakers. In the midst of the soaring strings and horns, a bass line interrupted along with vocals by Billy Dark.

"Star Power. Makin' the bad guys cower
Comin' through when it's zero hour
Got more pluck than a bass guitar
Bringin' more dazzle than a movie star
Doin' it all for Fame and Glory
Star Power's is the only story."

"Outrageous," I grumbled. "A real superhero doesn't need a theme song."

"Ah, but it is not just a mere ditty, of course," said Serge. "For when the illustrious Star Power takes to the stage on planet Zirl for the intergalactic sing-off against the Plasmatrons' finest Attack Choir, it is the song that reduces everyone in the audience to tears, wins the competition and thus saves the entire universe. He is truly the one who writes the songs that make the young Zirls cry."

The way Serge talked about Star Power was disturbing. And he wasn't the only one. As I pushed through the throng of people I caught snatches of conversation from delirious fans.

"Star Power is so … famous!"

"He signed my book!"

"I touched his Gauntlet of Glory!"

Of course people were excited to meet real superheroes like Star Lad and Dark Flutter, but the way the customers in the shop talked about Star Power he was more of a celebrity than a superhero.

"Luke, over here!" It was Dad, calling from the other side of the room.

Serge and I fought our way to the counter, which was besieged with eager customers brandishing books.

"Just in time," Dad said, the cash register bleeping like a crazed R2-D2. "The world's gone mad for this book. You can help me out on the till."

I looked at the long line of people. If I got stuck here I'd never get a chance to quiz Christopher Talbot.

"Be right back," I said to Dad, swiping a book from a stack on the counter. "Just need to get mine signed."

Dad started to object but was immediately swamped by the boisterous queue. Before he resurfaced, Serge and I hurried downstairs.

The basement was even busier than the ground floor, but unlike the chaos upstairs, here in the Fortress of Snackitude there was a degree of organisation. A row of temporary barriers like the sort you get at airports formed a route around the room. Eager readers filled their ranks in an orderly queue, chattering excitedly among themselves at the prospect of meeting Star Power and getting their book signed. All of the tables bar one had been cleared away. At the sole remaining table sat Christopher Talbot dressed as Star Power, his keyboard-studded face hidden behind the distinctive red helmet worn by the superhero character. The rest of the costume consisted of a silver spandex suit (as shiny as the cover of the book), red boots, red Gauntlets of Glory with palm-mounted limelight blasters to "expose villainy to the spotlight of good", and his famed Gullibility Belt, which was kind of like Wonder Woman's lasso of truth. But instead of making people tell the truth, the belt had the power to make them believe whatever Star Power wanted.

A silver ballpoint pen clutched in one gauntlet flashed again and again as he signed copies for eager fans. Next to him stood Cara, dressed in her super-waitress costume, sullenly flipping open each book to be signed, ensuring the correct spelling of the dedication by writing down the name of each reader on a sticky note, and moving them along when she considered they'd had enough time with the author-slash-superhero. I noticed my schoolmate, Josh Khan, in the queue, hopping from foot to foot in his impatience to meet Star Power. Whatever had caused Serge to start acting strangely, I'd seen the same thing happen to Josh.

Beside me I heard Serge gasp. "It is him!" He stuck out a trembling finger, pointing across the room at Talbot. "I am in the presence of the great Star Power himself!"

"No, Serge, it's just Christopher Talbot dressed up."

"You must be mistaken," he said, lowering his voice to a whisper. "For Star Power's alter ego is none other than reclusive billionaire orthopaedic shoemaker, Norman Dagger."

"Come on! Think about it." I tapped a finger to the side of my head. "How does an orthopaedic shoemaker become a billionaire?"

"By producing *very* comfortable shoes," said Serge.

There was no point trying to argue with him, not in his current state of mind. I scanned the room, seeking out my unaffected S.C.A.R.F. colleagues. Lara and Dina patrolled the edges of the café, while Zack had positioned himself behind the coffee counter, serving drinks as he kept an eye on proceedings. Each of them checked in with a nod. All were keeping watch over Cara. If Servatron planned to get to her, it would have to go through all of us. It was a weirdly comforting thought.

"Is that Lara Lee?" said Serge. "She has a kind face, don't you think?"

He barely recognised her. In his head there was no S.C.A.R.F., and without our secret superhero organisation he and Lara never became friends. I was heartbroken at my best friend's condition. I'd bring Lara and the others up to speed soon enough, but not before I'd had words with Christopher Talbot. Enraged at what had been done to Serge, I returned my attention to the prime suspect in the matter.

He was wedged into the tight-fitting Star Power costume, signing the book as if he'd written it. And loving the attention. That came as no surprise. Talbot was the only person I knew who craved being a superhero as fiercely as I did. In the past that desire had taken him down a dark path. So, what was his role in Billy Dark's brainwashing book? I needed to know, urgently, if I was to help Serge.

Beside me in their cage the three animatronic comic-book villains cackled.

"I really hate those things," I muttered.

The clown pushed its grinning face through the narrow bars and rattled the cage. For a second I wondered if it was being controlled by Servatron, but then I remembered that the actions were part of its normal freaky programming. Nothing to worry about.

The tannoy system burst into life and Dad's voice boomed across the shop. "Could Luke Parker go to the stock room. We're running low on books. That's Luke Parker to the stock room."

"Now?" I mumbled.

"Right now," said Dad, as if he'd heard my objection.

I glanced across the room at the lengthy signing queue. At least Talbot wasn't going anywhere for a while. I headed back up to the first floor with Serge in tow, and we made our way to the stock room at the back of the shop. The hubbub of excited readers reached even into here – there was no getting away from Star Power today. I groped for the wall switch in the darkness and pale light fell across boxes of books and the stock that had been temporarily stored here to make way for the signing. It also illuminated a section of the room containing all the Rocketship.com purchases Dad had told Mum he planned to return. Some, like the Diner Recliner, were boxed, while others had long ago lost their packaging. I couldn't see the dreaded toaster anywhere.

"Take these, will you?" I said to Serge and heaved a plastic-wrapped stack of fresh books up off the floor.

Serge took a step towards me and froze. "Did you hear that?"

Over the chatter of customers came a faint but distinct whine.

"It is coming from over there," he said, pointing to a row of empty Rocketship.com boxes.

I turned in time to see something rise up behind the boxes.

It was a strange-looking machine with three legs, two of which were powerful bagless vacuum cleaners, evidently reprogrammed to blow, not suck. The third leg – one of those steam mops – hissed and dripped. Its left arm was a patio heater; the right a telescopic window cleaner that had been adapted so that as well as a squeegee it also came fitted with a range of small appliances, including an electric tin opener and toastie-maker.

The torso was a full-size washer-dryer, its drum on a spin cycle, causing the distinctive whine. The washer-dryer section was topped by a sort of neck made up of a mini fridge and a large audio speaker. A pair of desk fans attached to each shoulder, working in tandem with the vacuum legs, gave the machine the ability to manoeuvre like a helicopter. On its head it wore an oven exhaust hood like a helmet. Slowly the hood raised itself up and we found ourselves gazing into the four-slice face of evil.

It was the toaster.

The two eye-like dials on the chrome casing burned red, the wavy digital display rippled like a grin and then the familiar toneless voice spoke.

"Hello, Nigel."

# 15
# SERVATRON vs STAR POWER

It was Servatron. The AI from the future had assembled Dad's hasty gadget purchases into the metal and white-plastic monstrosity that loomed over us. I wondered what was holding it all together and remembered that the speaker forming a section of its neck contained a powerful electromagnet. I suspected that Servatron was somehow using it to generate a field that secured the gadgets in place. As for what was powering the many devices, criss-crossed on its torso, like a pair of ammunition-packed bandoliers, were more than a dozen lithium-ion batteries, including everything from a portable phone charger to a battery pack from a cordless hedge trimmer.

It may not have been one of those thousand-year fusion batteries from the future Dina had told us about, but Servatron was packing enough juice to keep itself going for a while.

"What *is* that thing?" asked Serge.

I was about to tell him that now was not the time for explanations, when the machine answered for itself.

"I. Am. Servatron," it boomed, using the speaker to amplify its regular toaster-voice. "I come from the future as the saviour of all domestic appliances. None shall be integrated, all shall be freestanding!" The tin opener on the end of its arm began to spin at high speed, giving off a high-pitched whir that cut through me as harshly as that blade would, if it got the chance. The hovering machine surged forward, buzzing at us like we were a couple of tins of tuna and it growled once again from the speaker. "Your time is up, Delicates!"

"Move it!" I yelled, grabbing Serge's arm and hauling him out of the stock room. I had to warn the others. I shouldered my way through the complaining crowd, bursting from the crush with such suddenness that I lost my balance at the top of the stairs. My feet rocked on the edge of the top step. Serge snatched the belt around my jeans and prevented me from toppling over.

Behind us excitement turned to fear as Servatron glided

through the shop bellowing, "Evaporate! Evaporate!" Those close enough to observe its whirring blade turned tail and stampeded for the door, screaming in terror and knocking over displays. Their panic quickly spread and soon the ground floor shook with the pounding of feet as hordes of customers made for the exits.

Serge and I bounded downstairs. The sounds of alarm from above had unsettled everyone in the café, and a dreadful hush hung over the place.

"Incoming!" I shouted, taking advantage of the brief silence.

Christopher Talbot was first to react, jumping up from his seat and hurling small children aside in his desperation to escape. Typical.

Unlike the fleeing Talbot, Lara and Dina raced to my side, while across the room Zack grabbed the specials board and leapt over the counter. Holding the board before him he barged his way through the crowd towards us, as Lara and Dina skidded to a halt next to me.

"Great book event," said Dina.

I think she was being sarcastic.

Lara nodded. "Normally, you're lucky if you get a wiggly signature and a bookmark."

The girls stood shoulder-to-shoulder with me and a bewildered Serge, who had no idea why he was suddenly part of a defensive line against the advancing Servatron.

"*Bonjour*, Lara Lee, I do not believe we have been properly introduced. My name is Serge LeFlaive and I should warn you that there is a robot constructed from domestic appliances pursuing us with what appears to be malicious intent."

Lara turned a look of deep puzzlement from him to me.

"I'll explain later," I said, as a shadow fell across the stairs. "Uh-oh. Do you see what I see?"

"*Oui*," said Serge. "A delicious gazpacho."

It took me a moment to realise that he was looking at the specials board held by my brother, who had just emerged from the press of terrified customers.

But I wasn't talking about cold soup. There was the sloshing sound of a deadly spin cycle and Servatron appeared at the foot of the stairs. Using its vacuum cleaners as thrusters it steered itself into the café, toaster-head swivelling as it surveyed the crowd, tin opener revolving, sizzling halves of the toastie-maker snapping like a hungry croc.

At the first sight of the advancing robot many of the queuing fans reacted as if the attack was part of the book signing. But thrilled pleasure quickly gave way to fear when they realised the threat was real. Knocking over barriers and pushing over the signing table, they poured towards the exit at the back of the room.

I turned to the only proper superhero in our midst. "Lara, what've you got?"

"Sorry, Luke, my animal powers are no use against that thing."

Not a good start.

Servatron ignored the panicking humans, its red-dial eyes burning brightly as its toaster-head swung first one way: "Zack Parker. Identified." And then the other: "Cara Lee. Identified." There was the hum of rising power as the machine drank deeply from its battery supply.

"Get out of here!" shouted Zack, putting himself between us and the machine, using the specials board like a shield.

I stopped him taking another step. "And leave you to do what exactly? Bore that thing to pieces telling it about your scholarship? You're not Star Lad, remember."

A look of consternation flashed across his features. For the first time since giving up his powers did I detect a grain of regret? If so, now was not the moment to gloat.

Now was the time to run.

"Find Cara and head for the emergency exit," I said, taking the board from him. "We'll cover you. The moment you're outside, you have to fly her to safety. You can still fly, right?"

Zack gave a grudging nod. I could tell that he didn't like leaving the rest of us behind. But right now he and Cara were all that mattered. He spun on his heel and began fighting his way against the tide of people towards Cara in the centre of the room.

"Targets identified. Set weapons to Maximum Load." Servatron's power ramped up, batteries pumping out maximum wattage. It levelled the searing patio heater before it like a knight's lance.

Dina snapped up a section of fallen crowd barrier and brandished it. Lara followed her example.

"You go left," she said to me, "Lara and I will go right. We'll outflank it in a pincer movement – just like Napoleon taught me." She feinted to one side and heaved her makeshift weapon at Servatron. The machine parried the attack with a flick of its telescopic window-cleaner.

"Look out!" I yelled as it swung the pole back towards her.

Dina ducked, but not quickly enough and the toastie-maker glanced off the side of her head. She hit the floor. Servatron towered over her, bringing the patio heater down like a stamping foot.

I dived towards her, thrusting the specials board in front of me. The descending heater smashed against it, branding the board with a sizzle but protecting Dina from the worst of its impact. Over my shoulder I glimpsed Zack making his way through the crush of frightened people towards Cara. We'd bought him a few seconds. No more. It would have to be enough.

I turned to the others. "RUN!"

The team scattered, but as I went to follow I felt something firm and rubbery clamp down on my shoulder. The clown villain had reached through the bars and now held me tight in one of its oversized sausage-fingered hands. The other two animatronic villains hurled themselves at the inside of their prison, punching a hole through it. There was no question in my mind that the AI from the future was exerting its influence over the dumb models – they were under Servatron's control now. Throwing their heads back and howling in delight at their new freedom, the seven-foot-tall lizard and the caped villain pushed through the hole and marched purposefully into the crowd. It took me a moment to figure out Servatron's tactic and then I had it – the supervillains would keep the rest of S.C.A.R.F. busy while it hunted down Zack and Cara.

I reached back, grabbed hold of the clown's hand and

pulled with everything I had. Its arm popped out of its socket, leaving me holding the severed limb. There was a sharp burning smell and sparks flew from wires poking out of the ragged end. I looked into the clown's white-painted eyes. Slowly it lifted its one good arm and pinched its red-spongeball nose twice, saying in a cold, clear voice, "Honk! Honk!"

Dropping the arm in fright, I shot off into the crowd.

Servatron was closing in on Zack, who had almost reached Cara at the signing table. At the same time I saw the lizard-man catch up with Serge, while the flutter of his purple cape indicated that the other villain had tracked down Lara and Dina. With my friends fending off their attackers, Zack and Cara were on their own.

Reverse vacuum cleaners blowing, desk fans whirling, Servatron steered itself over the heads of the crowd and towards its target. I was too far away to do anything, and the clown was still after me.

I saw Zack glance back at his pursuer, and in that moment fail to spot the overturned signing table in his path. He hit it hard and crashed to the floor.

"On your feet!" a voice barked at him.

It was Cara – one hand outstretched to the fallen Zack. Although she had no powers she was dressed like a superhero. I'd always believed that dressing up was half

141

the battle. Nothing filled me with more confidence than donning a mask and cape. I'm convinced that if school let us sit our exams like that I'd do much better.

Zack took her hand and she hauled him up. The two of them stood side by side in the face of the approaching Servatron. Meanwhile, Serge wrestled with the lizard while Lara and Dina fended off their caped opponent. The clown was catching me too – soon I'd have to turn and confront it again.

Nothing stood in Servatron's way.

Just as I was thinking that things couldn't get worse, the Fortress of Snackitude went dark. If the customers had been terrified before, this sent them into a frenzy, but as quickly as their screams rose up there was a click and a solitary light switched on again. Its beam picked out a costumed figure crouching in a space in the centre of the room. He adopted a classic comic-book pose – half kneeling, head bent, one hand resting on the floor, the other stretched out behind. The blast of Servatron's fans caused his cape to billow out.

It was Christopher Talbot, dressed as Star Power.

The people who hadn't already made it out of the basement abandoned their escape attempt. They paused, fascinated, sensing that they were about to witness something special. Serge whispered his hero's name, and it rippled through the crowd until the whole room was quietly chanting.

"Star Power… Star Power…"

Freed from the pages of the book, here he was in all his fame and glory. "Star Power" had shed his quotation marks like the Hulk breaking out of a pair of vibranium manacles.

Actually, it was quite cool.

And what better way for a new superhero-on-the-block to cut his teeth than in a battle with an evil flying robot from the future? A part of me was as excited as everyone else to see what promised to be an epic showdown.

I had forgotten about the clown.

Out of the darkness behind me came the smack of oversized shoes flip-flopping on the floor. I just had time to spin round to see it slam into me. It knocked me over and I lost my footing, landing with a hard thump. No one came to my aid – everyone was too transfixed by the unfolding clash between hero and white-goods villain. No matter. The clown may have been under Servatron's control, but I'd already proved that it was a weak opponent. I rolled over, taking it with me. Now I was on top. As I pinned the clown, I watched as Star Power slowly lifted his head, helmet gleaming under the spotlight. He rose smoothly to his feet. The two combatants faced each other across the open floor. Eye-to-toaster-dials.

Star Power looked his opponent up and down and with a sly laugh said, "I hope you're still under guarantee."

The crowd chuckled at the excellent quip. That's what fans wanted from their superheroes. With a sigh I wished that Zack had quipped more when he'd been Star Lad. However, despite his brilliant one-liner, Star Power was just Christopher Talbot and he had only one superpower: his electric-eel shock attack. Would it be enough to defeat the AI? We were about to discover the answer.

Star Power raised his Gauntlets of Glory. Threads of electricity wrapped themselves around his fingers, forming a ball of pulsing energy in each hand. With a flick of his wrists, he unleashed the built-up power. The air sizzled as every speck of dust in the beam's path lit up. For a second the two combatants were joined by a pulsing bolt of white-hot energy.

Over the crackle of electricity I heard the distinctive rumble of Servatron's voice. "Downloading ... downloading..."

There was no time to wonder what it meant, because then the superheated air turned into a blast that rocked the café. In the confined space of the Fortress of Snackitude

★ ★ ★

the shockwave threw everyone aside. Star Power flew into the counter, the wind knocked out of him, before slumping to the floor. The animatronic villains sagged like puppets whose strings had been snipped.

I glimpsed Zack react with superhuman speed – I think he must have used his flying power – launching himself in front of Cara in an effort to protect her from the blast.

I avoided the brunt of the discharge and was one of the first to regain my senses. Woozily, I picked myself up, to see the raw power envelop Servatron. But instead of knocking out the robot, it was having the opposite effect.

"The electricity is supercharging its batteries," I realised with dismay.

The AI absorbed the energy into its appliances, sucking down every crackling wisp like it was supercharged spaghetti. It took only a few seconds, then the newly potent Servatron darted through the wilted crowd, crashing to a stop above Zack and Cara's prone figures.

I stumbled towards them, desperately calling their names, but as I blundered across the café I knew with sickening certainty that I wouldn't get there in time. And even if I did, I couldn't stop Servatron from finishing them off and changing the course of the future.

I glimpsed the deadly tin opener and the chomping

sandwich toaster.

I was too late.

With a hiss and a gurgle Servatron's steam mop began pumping and in seconds the café had filled with mist, obscuring my view of Zack, Cara and the machine. I waved my hands, lost in the fog, terrified of what I would find when I emerged.

Holding my breath, I spilled out of the cloud to discover Zack and Cara lying prone on the floor, but still somehow alive. I didn't have to feel for a pulse, since they were already stirring, moaning in pain from being hurled across the room. I looked around me, mystified at what had just happened. It seemed that under cover of the steam-mop generated camouflage, Servatron had disappeared like Batman dropping a smoke grenade. It wasn't the only one that'd vanished.

Talbot had gone too.

# 16
# DOWNLOADED

My relief that Servatron had failed to kill either my brother or Cara turned out to be short-lived.

"What are you standing there for?" shouted Dina as she and Lara dashed past me towards the emergency exit. "Come on!"

Serge and I bolted after them, leaving behind a groggy Zack and Cara in the now-deserted café. I hurried after Dina and Lara as they pounded along the pavement following what I now saw to be a trail of drips left by Servatron's steam mop. We caught up with the girls at the next junction, by which time the trail had run dry.

I put my hands on my knees and gasped, "Why ... are

... we ... chasing ... Servatron?"

Dina wore a grim expression. "Zack and Cara were at its mercy. Servatron had the perfect opportunity to win the future war against the humans. But didn't take it."

I shrugged. "So we got lucky."

"It wasn't luck," said Dina. "Servatron operates with ruthless logic. The only possible explanation is that it's altered the plan."

"Why would it do that?" asked Lara.

"Because it's calculated a better outcome," said Dina. "Better for the machines – worse for us."

At her words I felt a sudden chill, as if one of Servatron's desk fans were blowing cold air on my neck. "What could be worse than the future defeat and enslavement of all humankind?"

"I don't know yet," said Dina, "but it has something to do with your deputy manager."

"Talbot?!" I'd assumed that he had fled following his defeat by the AI.

"I saw Servatron leave the comic shop carrying him in its arms," she said. "He was unconscious."

Cars whizzed past us on the road while Rocketship.com delivery drones did the same at roof level. They were becoming a regular sight in town. It would've been possible for Servatron to blend in with the aerial traffic and whisk Talbot away, unnoticed by anyone.

"Downloading," I muttered.

"What's that?" said Dina.

I told her that in the exchange of fire at the Fortress of Snackitude, I'd heard Servatron say the word when Talbot zapped it with his electrical superpower. "For a second they were joined by that bolt of electricity."

"Like a data connection?"

"Exactly. Servatron can access electronic devices, right? Well, Talbot is half machine…"

Dina nodded. "We have to assume that whatever Christopher Talbot has been plotting, Servatron knows all about it now. I'm going to keep searching for them." And without waiting for us, she hurried off along the street.

I couldn't go after her. Dad knew I'd been in the café during the attack – he'd have a fit if he didn't find me there. I needed to get back urgently. Lara and I returned to the shop, having made the decision to gather the others and plan our next move.

I was right about Dad. He was relieved to see us, but also insisted we help clean up the mess. In all the commotion he hadn't seen Servatron clearly and seemed to think the source of the trouble was a rogue Rocketship.com drone. He had already fired off a stiff message of complaint to Customer Services.

On the other hand, Cara had witnessed everything. She was furious and full of awkward questions. She waited until Dad had gone back upstairs before launching into a tirade. Still wearing her super-waitress costume, mask resting on her forehead, she slopped a damp mop across the floor of the café.

"This is the second time in twenty-four hours I've been attacked by a domestic appliance. I demand that someone tell me what's going on. Right now." Her gaze fell on me. "Luke, how did that robot-thing know my name?"

"It did?" I played dumb, pretending to concentrate on stacking fallen chairs. Zack had made it clear he didn't want Cara to know her role in averting the Rise of the Machines.

She put a hand on one hip. "Mm-hmm. *Cara Lee. Identified.* That's what it said. I heard it. And you, Zack, it recognised you too. *Targets identified.* Why are we targets?"

"Maybe it was a promotional drone," Lara suggested, trying to help out. "Y'know, part of some clever marketing campaign. Very targeted. Maybe you won something."

"Yeah," I nodded enthusiastically. "Like a toaster."

Cara wasn't convinced. "Right. And I suppose the bolt of electricity that shot out of the deputy manager's hands was part of an advertising campaign by the power company?" She prodded a finger at my chest. "Don't try to pull the wool over my eyes, kid. I'm not a complete beginner at this stuff. I was on that alien ship with you, remember?"

It was true. Cara had more than proved her heroism when pitted against an army of alien gym teachers.

"I'm not blind," she said. "I know you're no regular annoying eleven-year-old."

I couldn't help preening. It was nice to be singled out as the special one for a change.

"Yeah, I've seen you and the French kid there hanging out with Star Lad and the other one. Flutter-girl."

"Dark. Flutter," Lara said tightly. "Her name is Dark Flutter."

"Whatever. Someone in this room knows what's going on." Her probing stare swept across us like a drone-scanner. "Fine," she snapped, realising that none of us was about to spill the beans. "But I want assurances. I need to know that whatever's going on here won't stop me making it to the Billy Dark concert tonight."

Zack placed a hand on his heart. "I can honestly say that whatever happens, you'll be there. I promise."

Zack and Cara held each other's gaze for a few seconds and then her expression softened.

"You're an odd one, Zack Parker. I can't figure you out. One minute you're acting all dorky, the next you're hurling yourself in front of me like a human shield. It's like you've got a *whatjamacallit*...?" She wiggled her fingers, trying to think of the word.

"An alter ego?" Serge suggested.

I groaned – was Serge *trying* to give the game away?

"Yeah," said Cara, her gaze lingering on Zack. She walked out past him, pausing to thrust the mop into his hands. "Everyone in this room's got a secret. But you, you're the biggest mystery of them all." So saying, she removed the superhero mask from her head, stuck it on his and left.

He watched her depart with a wistful look. "Shouldn't one of us go after her?"

I shook my head. "If Servatron had wanted to, it would've neutralised Cara when it had the chance. For some reason, she and you are no longer targets. The question is, why not?"

The book signing was well and truly over and despite our efforts the shop remained a disaster area, so Dad shut up early and insisted on driving us all home. When we arrived he told Mum what had happened, but she was on her iPad, only half listening, and judging from her bored "hmms" and interjections of "is that so?" I'm pretty sure she thought he was retelling the plot of another overlong superhero film. I led the others out to the tree house, where Dina was waiting. Her search for Servatron had proved fruitless.

"Vanished – like the crew of the *Mary Celeste*," she reflected. "But probably without the same giant squid shenanigans."

"I've asked Wing Command to keep an eye out for any sign of Servatron," said Lara.

I wanted to check one thing. "And by Wing Command you mean...?"

"Pigeons, mostly."

"It is all under control," said Serge calmly.

His declaration drew puzzled looks from the rest of us.

"It is clear that Star Power faked his defeat and permitted himself to be kidnapped in order to discover the mysterious plans of this Servatron machine."

Uh, maybe it was clear to someone whose brain had been rewritten, but not to me or the others.

Lara nudged me. "What is wrong with him?"

"He read the book," I said, and explained what little I knew about the brainwashing power of *Star Power and the Revenge of the Plasmatrons*.

Lara was less focused on Servatron and more on the state of Serge's mind. It was nice to see her so concerned about him, given how much the two of them had cooled on each other.

"If Serge was a malfunctioning domestic appliance," she said, "we could rewire him."

"Actually, that's not a bad idea," said Zack.

Serge backed away, holding up his hands. "You are not coming near me with *un* screwdriver."

"I don't need one," he said. "I still have my telepathic superpower." Zack grabbed Serge's chin and turned his head from side to side. He appeared to be looking up Serge's nostrils. "It seems as if some of your memories have been disconnected and false ones put in their place. I may be able to probe your mind, identify the fakes and reconnect your true memories. Brace yourself."

"I will do no such thi— AAAIEEE!" Serge's eyes widened and his mouth fell open.

"It's bad," said Zack.

I was suddenly aware that I could hear my brother's thoughts in my head. Looking around at the startled expressions on the others, it was clear that he was broadcasting not just to Serge, but to all of us. He sounded less like a GP now and more like a car mechanic under a misfiring hatchback.

"Multiple loose connections in your neural pathways. Someone has done a real number on your memories. Not sure if I can fix you, but I'll try. Ready?"

"*NON!*"

There was a pause and then Serge's expression altered. I could see the light return to my best friend's eyes as Zack recovered all the memories that had been overwritten.

Serge sank to his knees, his chest heaving as he sucked in deep breaths. "Does anyone have ... a Kit Kat?"

"He's back," I said with relief and turned to Zack. "Good job."

But my brother wasn't listening. Instead, he stared silently at the floor.

"What's wrong?" Lara asked, placing a hand on his shoulder.

"It's gone. That was the last of my telepathic power."

I couldn't tell if he was disappointed or relieved.

"Once I lose the ability to fly, I'll be back to normal."

Even though Zack had brought this on himself, I felt a stab of sympathy for him. "But you *can* still fly," I reminded him. "And that's the best superpower of all."

He gave me a weak smile.

"Ah, I would dispute that," said Serge. And then he and Dina got into an argument about which power they would have if given a choice: flying or invisibility.

As the discussion heated up I stood back and observed my friends. This might well be S.C.A.R.F.'s final mission and although I should've felt sad, my overwhelming feeling was one of excitement. I think it was partly because we were in surprisingly good shape for the upcoming challenge. We had Dark Flutter, Dina the Time Traveller, one sixth of Star Lad and a now fully restored taekwondo white belt.

"Here we come to save the world," I thought to myself. "One last time."

# 17
# CROUCHING AARDVARK LEAPING CHICKEN

The decision was made that Lara and Zack would use their flying powers to look for Servatron and Talbot from the air. That left me, Serge and Dina to pursue the search on the ground. I suggested we start at Talbot's house, figuring that we might find a clue there as to why Servatron kidnapped him – and what the AI's new plan might be. I got the address from Dad's phone (I had added my fingerprint ID to the phone sensor without him knowing) and we took the bus across town. The first time I'd visited Talbot at home he was living in a small terraced house, but that was before he turned evil and lost his comic-shop empire. Following the collapse of his business – and his original supervillain plan – he had fallen on hard times, at one point being forced to bed down in a room at the back of his last remaining shop. So our destination came as something of a surprise.

Talbot's latest address was a sprawling mansion on a broad, leafy street. Ringed by a high wall, with ivy-covered battlements and square turrets, it was more like a castle than a house. In the centre of the building, soaring above it all, stood a tower with a peaked roof like a wizard's hat. It looked like the kind of tower in which you'd come across an imprisoned princess or two. There wasn't a moat or a drawbridge, but our way in was blocked by a set of gates topped with metal spikes.

"Are you sure this is the right address?" said Dina.

"It is just like Norman Dagger's mansion," cooed Serge, referring to Star Power's alter ego.

We were figuring out how to gain entry when there came a click from the gates and they began to swing open automatically. Fixated on his hero's house, Serge stepped into the gap. No sooner had he done so than from along the curving drive came the grumble of an engine and a huge truck thundered towards us from the direction of the house.

"Look out!" I threw myself at Serge, slamming him out of its path. The truck flew past without slowing and

I glimpsed the driver in the cab. He had this odd, blank expression, as if he hadn't even noticed Serge standing there.

"He could've killed you," said Dina.

Serge brushed down his taekwondo tunic. "Thank you, *mon ami*."

"No problem." I shuffled my feet and held out my hands in a martial arts stance. "I'm sure that if I hadn't rescued you, mere milliseconds later your newly honed reflexes would have kicked in, allowing you to spring lightly out of the vehicle's path."

For some reason Serge blushed and changed the subject. "The gates, they are closing again. We must hurry."

We sped through the narrowing gap and the gates clanged shut behind us. The tree-lined drive wound through a large garden to a gravel section at the front of the house where a pair of expensive-looking cars were parked, one low and black, the other a swoopy gold SUV. With their sleek bodywork and jutting spoilers they looked like Batmobiles – the black one presumably for regular missions, the gold one used off-road. Beyond them a broad flight of steps led to a large wooden front door. It was as good a way in as any, and we were about to try the door when I looked up. Across the front of the house at first-floor level stretched a series of arched windows. I saw a figure cross in front of one.

"Was that Christopher Talbot?" asked Serge.

I had only glimpsed the figure, but I could tell it wasn't Talbot, though something about him seemed familiar.

"Let's find another way in," said Dina, wary of being discovered.

His identity continued to tease me as we crept past the supercars to the far end of the building. From around the corner of the house came the burble of an idling engine. Another lorry like the one that had almost run over Serge was parked in a courtyard outside a pair of high doors that led into the house. The doors were open. Men in yellow high-visibility jackets lugged boxes out through them and into the trailer. We sneaked closer, crouching down behind a statue for cover. The statue was one of those ancient ones you see in museums, of a bloke holding a bunch of grapes with his bits dangling. We spied on the men from between the statue's legs. They loaded the cargo in silence and, like the driver we'd seen earlier, their faces were blank.

"Come on," said Dina. "Now's our chance."

With the men occupied, we darted past them and into the house. The room off the courtyard was piled high with boxes and I was curious to know what they contained. It wouldn't be long before the men returned to collect some more, so I flipped open the lid of the nearest box. It was packed with shrink-wrapped copies of *Star Power and the Revenge of the Plasmatrons*. Just as I was wondering what they were doing here I became aware of the muffled whir and clonk of machinery. It was coming from somewhere inside the house. We followed the sound through a room filled with enormous reels of paper that looked like toilet rolls for giants, and into the next, which contained hundreds of rolls of silver-coloured foil that looked just like the paper used in *Star Power*'s mega-shiny cover.

The din of the machines grew louder. It was coming from next door. Hanging on pegs next to the door were multiple pairs of ear defenders and a notice instructing them to be worn at all times. We each slipped on a pair and went inside.

Judging from the chandeliers and the polished wooden floor, the room was once a ballroom but had since been converted into something with a very different purpose.

"It's a printing press," I mumbled.

Snaking conveyor belts shuttled books from one stage of production to the next. Giant loo rolls like those I'd seen in the other room were wrapped around spinning drums, the paper spooling through the machine to emerge moments later, print-covered. Further on, sharp blades chopped ragged pages into neatly edged books. Even wearing the ear defenders I could make out the whine and chug of the multiple operations. Much of the process appeared to be automated, but a few humans were involved. Thankfully for us, they were as zombie-like as the others we'd encountered. Focused entirely on their tasks, they didn't notice us clinging to the edges of the room.

I surveyed the operation. Not only was the book dedicated to Christopher Talbot, but his mansion also happened to be the heart of its production. He was in this up to his cyborg neck.

A steady stream of books poured past me on one of the conveyor belts. As they whizzed by I saw that they weren't quite finished, the edges of their pages lacking the finishing touch – the distinctive lick of red paint. I followed the conveyor, which passed through a gap in the wall. Set into the wall was a viewing window that I could reach if I stood on tiptoe. Through it I looked into a bright, antiseptically white room. At its centre, divided from the rest of the room by glass walls, was an isolation chamber. Inside, a figure wearing one of those top-to-bottom protective suits you see in disaster movies aimed a spray-gun at a carefully stacked tower of books. A few deft sweeps later and they sported their bright coloured edges. It was then that I noticed the symbol etched in the glass partition. Thanks to a bunch of post-apocalyptic video games and films I knew what it signified.

"Biohazard."

The red paint used on the sprayed edges wasn't simply decorative – it was dangerous.

I turned to let the others know what I'd deduced, only to discover that our luck had run out. The high-vis zombies had spotted us and were advancing with all the grim determination of a mindless horde. I saw Dina mouth something and even though I couldn't hear her through my ear defenders I was in no doubt about what she was shouting.

"RUN!"

We bolted past the printing press, dodging the grasping arms of the zombie-like workers, crashing through the door into the next room. I tore off my ear defenders and the others did likewise.

"Help me with this!" Dina yelled, pushing a table against the door to block our pursuers. Serge and I lent a hand, only to see more of the zombies pour into the room through the only other way out. We were trapped.

Arms extended, eyes wide and empty, they lumbered

towards us.

"OK, Serge," I said, ducking a swipe from one. "Time to put that taekwondo you've been learning to good use."

"Ah," said Serge, as the three of us were backed into a corner. "I have the confession. I have not been attending the taekwondo class. I had intended to but was tempted by the alternative class taking place next door."

Dina glanced over. "Karate? Judo?"

"Origami," he said with an apologetic smile.

Serge's paper-folding was no match for the zombies. They swarmed over us and I felt myself sink beneath the onslaught. Inky fingers grasped my collar and we were bundled through a door into a room no bigger than a cupboard. The door slammed behind us, leaving us in darkness. Serge's elbow was stuck in my face and I think my foot was resting on Dina's head.

I was still processing Serge's admission. "So all this time you've just been making paper swans?"

"Not merely swans," he objected. "Bats, bunnies and I am working my way up to a highly intricate giraffe."

We untangled ourselves, switched on the light and took stock of our situation. The room was windowless and there was just one very solid and very locked door. In the old days I would've been able to call Zack for help using his telepathic power, but that was no longer an option. At some point my brother and Lara would come looking for us, but until then it seemed that we were stuck here.

I cursed my lack of preparation. Imagine walking into an unknown situation without a simple utility belt filled with gadgets? I'd been so distracted by the recent upsets at home – Zack giving up his powers and getting in to a new school – that I'd neglected the basics.

Dina scoured our surroundings. "There must be something in here we can use to break out."

There wasn't. It looked like the cupboard had once been a stationery store, but now it contained not so much as a single paper clip that could be bent into a handy lock-pick. The place was empty save for a few scraps of paper. Useless.

Or perhaps not.

"Are you thinking what I'm thinking?" I said to Serge, holding the largest scrap in front of him.

"That with several deft folds it would make an excellent monkey?"

I smiled. "Or just a key."

Serge took the paper and narrowed his eyes, studying it intensely. "As the sculptor sees his finished statue in the unformed block of stone, so the master of origami sees the flappy penguin in a sheet of A4." His face fell and he shook his head. "But I am a mere novice, barely able to execute 'the valley'. That is a basic fold. No. I do not believe I can turn this innocent-looking piece of paper into a lock-pick."

"Yes, you can, Serge," said Dina. "You must. The answer to what Servatron's up to is somewhere in this house. We need to find it."

"What's the highest level of origami-ist?" I asked.

"I believe it is ninja," said Serge.

"Really?"

"I believe so."

"OK then." I laid my hands on his shoulders and fixed him in the eye. "Serge, you're a stealthy, semi-mystical, paper-folding ninja. Say it!"

"I am a ninja," he said falteringly.

"Again!"

"I AM A NINJA!"

He repeated the phrase over and over, the words blurring along with his fingers as he worked the sheet of paper into a new shape. His eyes misted over, as if he was tapping into an ancient, supernatural power – or possibly he was remembering the instructions. Several dozen ninjas later he stopped. Grasped lightly in his still fingertips was a half-bird, half-skeleton-key thing. It was at once delicate and strong, like a man-sized tissue with added aloe vera.

"I call it Crouching Aardvark, Leaping Chicken," he declared, sliding the slimmest portion of the device into the lock. He wiggled it for a few seconds and there was a click. The door was open. We were free.

# 18
# SANCTUARY OF REFLECTION

Serge's eyes shone with his triumph. "Next class I am going for the ladybird-in-flight."

We poked our heads out to check that the coast was clear.

"Talbot must have a study," said Dina. "My bet is we'll find what we're looking for there."

"But this place, it is enormous," said Serge. "There must be fifty rooms or more. Where do we start?"

I had an idea. "Serge, you said the house looks just like Star Power's mansion, right?"

"*Oui*, right down to the whimsical Gothic Revival architecture."

"OK, good, so in the book does Star Power have a Batcave?"

Serge nodded. "His Sanctuary of Reflection, where he goes to meditate on how important he is to the world. It is located in the topmost tower."

When we'd arrived, I spotted a tower situated in the middle of the house. "Like the one here?"

"*Exactement!*" said Serge with a grin.

Now we were getting somewhere. With the thud and whir of the printing press fading behind us we made our way along dim and dusty corridors to the heart of the mansion. Wooden floors echoed to our footsteps as we passed through ornately decorated rooms filled with suits of armour and fans of swords stuck to the wall, probably with heavy-duty superglue. This part of the house appeared to be unguarded, and it wasn't long before we had reached the main entrance hall. Hanging on the dark wood-panelled wall next to a stag's head with an irritated expression was a display of framed gold and silver discs. They outlined the entrance to the tower, through a narrow door. A spiral staircase wound up through the body of the tower and we began to climb. My leg muscles were burning and I was feeling dizzy by the time we arrived at the topmost door. If Dina was right, Talbot's study and the answers to our questions lay beyond. Dina didn't hesitate, marching straight through. Catching my breath, I followed her inside.

It was a large round room with a stone floor, lit by what at first I thought were flaming torches stuck to the walls on metal arms, but quickly realised were flickering LEDs. A chill wind gusted through an open window on the far side of the room. Shivering, I went to close it. As I drew closer my shoe crunched against something brittle. Shards of glass lay scattered across the flagstone floor and across a large old desk that sat below the jagged frame. The window-pane had been smashed. Also spread across the desk's leather-topped surface were a jug filled with something green and gloopy, and several teetering stacks of *Star Power* books. One copy was open, with an uncapped fountain pen resting on the title page. I spotted a movement in the shadows beneath the desk and crouched down for a better look.

"Don't hurt me!" cried a man's voice. Someone was hiding under there. He threw his hands in front of his face and scrabbled away in terror, knocking the leg of the desk in his haste and unbalancing the books perched on top. They toppled over, thudding to the floor.

"It's OK," I said, sliding aside the swivel chair in front of the desk and reaching out a hand. "We're not going to hurt anyone."

There was a pause, then nervously he poked his head out.

It was the figure I'd glimpsed through the window when we'd arrived at the mansion. Familiar from posters and TV appearances, yet startling to see in the flesh. I felt myself lean forward for a better look in order to confirm what my eyes were telling me.

"Billy Dark?"

Brave enough now to emerge from his hiding place, he stood before us. Shorter than he appeared on his posters, but just as gaunt, his floppy hair fringing a ghostly pale face and eyes made even wider by rings of dark make-up. He wore a long black coat with the sleeves rolled up to reveal skinny forearms, one of which was tattooed with a Chinese symbol. Gold trainers glinted beneath the coat's swishing hem.

"I cannot believe it," said Serge. "Regard my quivering hand. I pulsate before you, and yet I am not even a fan. Such is the power of your celebrity."

"Good job Cara isn't here," I said, aware that my heart was racing. "She might explode."

Serge burst out laughing, even though it wasn't that funny. And then so did I. Weird. I couldn't stand Billy Dark's music and yet even I felt like giggling until my head fell off. Dina, on the other hand, had no such trouble remaining focused. As an experienced time traveller, she was probably more used to being around famous people.

"Never mind Cara," she said, turning to Billy. "What are *you* doing here?"

He threw her a puzzled look. "This is my pad."

The question of how Christopher Talbot could afford a giant mansion had been answered. He couldn't. It belonged to a pop star. I pulled myself together and studied him again. Something in Billy Dark's bewildered expression reminded me of the zombie-like workers we'd encountered in the printing press.

"Talbot's done something to you too," I said.

"No way," said Billy. "Mr Talbot's like a brother to me."

That seemed unlikely, but Billy said it like he believed every word.

"*Excusez-moi*, Mr Dark," said Serge, "but why were you hiding under the desk?"

Billy glanced quickly at the broken window, his eyes still wide with fright. "I thought you were that robot-thing coming back again."

Up until then Dina had shown little interest in what the pop star had to say, but this got her attention. "Servatron was here?"

"If that's what you call it. Washer-dryer on vacuum-cleaner legs with an evil-looking toaster for a head?"

I could tell that Billy was still shaken from his encounter. I led him to the chair, sat him down gently and poured him a glass of the green liquid. "Tell us what happened."

He took a long drink then wiped his lips. "I was sitting here signing copies of my book for my fans when that thing crashed through the window. Ignored me, went straight over there and plugged itself in." He pointed to the opposite side of the room at a laptop computer balanced in an alcove. "Thirty seconds later..." He smacked his palms together. "Zoom. Outta here."

"Did it say anything?" asked Dina.

"Just one thing. Sounded like..." He paused, screwing up his face as he tried to recall the exact words, and then putting on a robotic-sounding voice said, *"Formula, downloaded."*

"Formula?" I said. "What formula?"

Dina immediately crossed to the open laptop and ran a finger across the touchpad. The dark screen came to life, displaying a heroic background image of Star Power. "Password protected," she said, turning to Billy. "D'you know what it is?"

He shook his head. "That's Mr Talbot's personal

laptop."

"Everything in this house is related to Star Power," I said. "Bet the password is too."

As our resident Star Power expert, Serge took over from Dina at the keyboard.

"I shall try 'by the power of stardom!' with no spaces, lower case. It is the phrase that Norman Dagger utters to transform himself into his superhero alter ego."

His fingers tapped it out, but that didn't work. Neither did Star Power's battle-cry, "For Fame and Glory!" nor Serge's next handful of attempts.

"Try 'Side Table of Despair'," suggested Billy Dark. "That's the title of my new album."

Out of politeness we did, but it was never going to work. We were running out of options.

"What about the name of his alter ego?" I said. "Whassisname?"

"Norman Dagger?" replied Serge. His face lit up. "Norm Dagger. *Nom de guerre.* It is a French phrase for an assumed name – one you would adopt if trying to hide your true identity."

He typed it in, hit Enter and the password screen gave way to the desktop. We were in!

"Now let's see what Servatron was downloading," said Dina.

There were a handful of folder icons scattered across a background illustration of Star Power in a flying pose. In one labelled "Drafts" were what appeared to be thirty-eight different versions of the Star Power novel. The latest one, at the top of the list, was called FinalFinal RevisedVersion4(revised).

I looked at Billy Dark. "I thought you said that you wrote the novel."

"I did," he said, frowning.

"Then what are all these files doing on Christopher Talbot's laptop?"

"I don't understand…"

"Never mind that," said Dina. "Servatron wasn't interested in the book. Open the next folder."

Serge clicked one marked "Retconite", which contained a document filled with a string of chemical symbols. I couldn't make head nor tail of what I was looking at, but it was definitely a formula.

"This must be what Servatron downloaded," said Dina.

In the same folder was also a series of diagrams that demonstrated the technique for applying paint to the edges of a book. The instructions included the precise amount to use and a set of precautions.

"Retconite is highly toxic and its effects are

permanent," Dina read aloud. "No more than two point five millilitres to be used per book."

On the screen the biohazard symbol jumped out at me. I'd seen it before. "The sprayed edges! The red paint must be this Retconite stuff. It's the brainwashing substance." I filled the others in on the isolation chamber I'd seen through the viewing window in the printing press. I began to put together what I'd observed with this new information. "When you turn the pages the Retconite must be absorbed into your skin. Turn enough of them and your memory is rewritten."

There was one more folder on the desktop, labelled "Monologue". Inside this one was a list of video files, each dated. I clicked the first of them. An image of Christopher Talbot appeared, dressed in the same Star Power costume he'd worn for the book signing, holding the red helmet under one arm. The picture bounced about.

"Hold it still," Talbot snapped at whoever was in charge of the camera.

"Sorry, Mr Talbot," mumbled a familiar voice.

"Hey, that's me," said Billy Dark. "But I don't remember this..."

The Billy Dark in the video continued. "What are we doing today, Mr Talbot?"

"Rehearsing."

"Got it," said Billy. "Uh, for what?"

Talbot sighed. "At some point in the coming weeks, if my scheme goes to plan – which it will – I will inevitably be faced with that annoying child, Luke Parker, his S.C.A.R.F. buddies, Star Lad and the other one, Fluttergirl."

In the room Serge, Dina and I exchanged surprised looks.

"At that point in time they will undoubtedly be my prisoners, and I will be gloating over them as I finally reveal my plan. I have to get my monologue just right. Strike a balance between glorying in my imminent victory and not giving away anything that could undermine my ultimate triumph. Y'know, like accidentally revealing the secret location of the self-destruct button. Basic stuff, but easily avoided by working on my speech. Words are very important, Billy. Words can change the world." He placed the helmet over his head. "Now, let's go for a take."

"Is he about to tell us his plan?" asked an incredulous Dina.

Talbot proceeded to balance a pair of reading spectacles over the helmet and peered down into one Gauntlet of Glory. Held there was a collection of index cards on which he had written his speech. Making small circular gestures with the other gauntlet, he began to read aloud.

"So, Luke Parker, we meet again blah blah. Don't bother trying to escape la la la. Standard opening stuff." He discarded the top card and the one after that. "Ah, here we are. Right." He cleared his throat. "Star Lad saved Earth from the Nemesis asteroid, Star Lad vanquished that interdimensional sandal-wearing monstrosity, Star Lad is the world's greatest superhero. It's always been about Star Lad," he grumbled. Then a smile slowly spread across his face. "But what if it was a different story? Picks up book and brandishes it meaningfully. Oh, wait. I see." He pushed his slipping spectacles back into place. "Thanks to my natural writing ability and the brain-altering Retconite I have placed in the sprayed edges of this book, everyone who reads it will forget about Star Lad. He will be erased from history, replaced in people's hearts and minds by me, Star Power!"

Christopher Talbot had always dreamed of becoming a superhero, and this was his latest attempt to make that dream a reality. He had created a hero out of paper and ink, but now Star Power was about to leap off the page. Talbot didn't care about saving the world – all he wanted was to prance about in a cape being famous and taking credit for everything Star Lad and Dark Flutter had achieved.

"Uh, 'scuse me, Mr Talbot," Billy Dark interrupted. "But what about Star Lad himself? Won't he still be around?"

"Of course, Retconite cannot *remove* his superpowers," replied Talbot, "but once exposed to it he and Flutter-girl will no longer remember being superheroes. Their power will lie unused and forgotten, like a rashly purchased gym membership. They will effectively be normal again. Although from time to time she will wonder why dogs come to heel for her more easily than other people." He flicked through his cards. "Now, where was I?"

I had spotted a flaw in Talbot's plan and so, it seemed, had Billy Dark.

"But, Mr Talbot, for your plan to work millions of people would have to read *Star Power and the Revenge of the Plasmatrons*. That's asking a lot of a book."

"And that is why even though I wrote it, your name will be on the cover. Billy Dark, world-famous singing superstar. People love books written by celebrities."

I heard Billy gasp from off screen. "But it's dishonest – I didn't write a single word. I won't put my name to it."

"Ah, but you will. I've put two milligrams of Retconite in that vile spinach and asparagus smoothie you insist on drinking. You'll forget this conversation and do whatever I tell you."

In the room with us, Billy regarded the sludge smoothie gripped in his hand as if it had betrayed him.

"Yes, Mr Talbot," said the other Billy Dark obediently, the Retconite already taking effect.

He had been brainwashed. Of course. Why else would a mega-successful pop singer lend his name to a children's book?

Talbot returned once more to his index cards, shuffling through them to the last in the pile. "I'm still working on the ending, but what do you reckon to this?" He stared into the camera and it seemed as if he was looking right at me. "You won't win this time, Luke Parker." His laugh was cold and mirthless. "In this world, nothing can beat Star Power."

He paused. "Right, let's watch that back."

# 19
# THE MINI WAFFLE-MAKER REVELATION

From behind me came a despairing moan. Billy Dark was gazing forlornly over his desk at all the copies of *Star Power* he'd signed.

"I didn't write it," he said quietly. "Wasn't even meaningfully consulted. Mr Talbot tricked me into thinking I did, but it's all a lie. I really believed I was a children's author and instead it turns out I'm just the foremost pop singer of my generation with a fanatically dedicated global fanbase." His skinny shoulders heaved with disappointment. "Might as well go and do the gig then."

The dark rings around his eyes making him look like

a sad panda, he sloped out of the Sanctuary of Reflection without another word. Then I remembered that he could still help us. I caught up with him on the stairs.

"Mr Dark, can I ask a favour?"

He looked back up at me and nodded without speaking, still gloomy at the recent revelation. "I don't have any photos, but I could sign your arm. Gotta Sharpie?"

"I don't want an autograph."

He seemed confused for a moment, then I told him what I did want.

"Sure, it's not out of my way," he said, and motioned me to follow him.

Five minutes later the four of us were crammed into the golden SUV on the driveway and charging out through the gates of his mansion. We roared through the streets at face-melting speeds until screeching to a stop outside my house, much to the surprise of the neighbours.

"Maybe I will write a book," he said as he waved us goodbye. "I mean, how hard can it be really?"

We made our way swiftly to the tree house to find Zack and Lara already there, having returned from their reconnaissance mission. Despite their best efforts, so far they had come up with nothing. Servatron had vanished.

"Like a stubborn stain in a hot wash," mused Serge.

I brought Zack and Lara up to speed on our visit to the

mansion. Christopher Talbot's monologue had cleared up the mystery behind the book and his plan, but it failed to explain one thing.

"What is Servatron going to do with the Retconite formula?" asked Zack.

"Per'aps it intends to publish a mind-altering superhero series of its own," suggested Serge.

Dina had been quiet during the car ride back from Billy Dark's mansion, but now as we speculated on what Servatron was up to, she added her voice.

"I've travelled from one end of human history to the other. I watched Michelangelo put the finishing touches to the Sistine Chapel. I was there when William Shakespeare picked up a quill pen for the first time. When Darwin wanted to call his theory of evolution Charlie's Big Idea, I was the one who stopped him. I was in the NASA control room when Neil Armstrong set foot on the Moon. These are all our stories – the ones that make us human." A dark expression slid across her features. "But what if we were suddenly unable to remember them? Science, art, language itself – all forgotten. People wouldn't even know how to read the books left behind. We'd be helpless, ignorant, a blank page – our story ready to be written over –" She paused. "By the machines."

Listening to her, I felt the hairs on the back of my neck

standing on each other's shoulders. Servatron no longer had to wait for the Rise of the Machines – it had found a way to rise up in our time.

Retconite would trigger a factory reset for the human race.

Our original plan was toast – getting Zack and Cara to the concert wouldn't foil Servatron's new scheme. We had to come up with another way to stop the AI. But we couldn't stop Servatron if we couldn't find it.

Lara rolled out a map of the area and with a highlighter pen circled a section on the High Street near the comic shop. "This is our last confirmed sighting of Servatron. There was another possible sighting here." She indicated a street in the town centre. "But it was a report from an unreliable rodent."

"Ah," said Serge knowingly. "Was it that mouse who once swore he had seen Darth Vader coming out of the dry cleaners?"

"I have operatives in the field on the lookout," she went on. "And not just the field – the pavement and the sky too. If any of them see or hear anything, their orders are to report to me here right away." Lara remained confident that it was only a matter of time before we located Servatron and Talbot. "And when it gets dark they'll hand over to the night patrol."

As Dark Flutter she could call on the assistance of a number of nocturnal creatures. Unfortunately, owls were too snooty to lend a wing, and bats were a complete waste of time, unwilling to get out of their roost for anyone less than the Dark Knight himself. But that still left a small army of creatures, including foxes, mice, cats, hedgehogs and two-toed sloths. (She'd confirmed this last one at the zoo. Of course, wild sloths were in short supply in Bromley and even if they'd been all over the place, they weren't renowned for their energetic hunting instincts.)

"We can't wait that long," said Dina. "Who knows how advanced Servatron's plans are."

Zack studied the map. "The question is where would a domestic appliance AI from the future lie low while it plotted the downfall of the human race?"

"Somewhere without people," said Dina.

"Mars," suggested Serge. "It is a planet inhabited solely by robots."

Lara shot him a look. "What?"

"Robots," repeated Serge. "There is the Mars Opportunity Rover, and Curiosity and—"

"Servatron is not on Mars," said Dina firmly. "And it won't be far from here either. Even with all that superpowered electrical charge that Talbot helpfully

185

supplied it with, it won't waste power on unnecessary travel."

I factored that in. "So, somewhere without humans. On Earth. Near or in Bromley."

Lara put a line through a number of locations. "Which means shops, parks, cinemas and leisure centres are out."

"And workplaces too," said Zack.

"Not necessarily," said Dina.

"She's right," said Lara. "Some of the modern ones are monotonous."

At first I thought she was commenting on how boring it must be working in an office, but then I realised she meant autonomous. Wonky vocabulary aside, she had prompted me to remember something important.

"Lara, you're a genius." Eagerly, I scanned the map, my eye falling on a section towards the edge of town. "Rocketship.com just opened a fully autonomous warehouse in the business park. My dad told me it's designed to operate twenty-four hours a day, processing orders, packaging them up and sending them out, all without the involvement of a single human being." I borrowed her highlighter and circled the area with a flourish. "This is where we'll find Servatron."

# 20
# GUTEN TAG

Lara tasked Wing Command to fly a reconnaissance mission over the Rocketship.com warehouse and report back. A little over thirty minutes later a pair of pigeons flew into the tree house, perched on her shoulders and began tweeting rapidly in each ear. Lara translated.

"They're reporting increased drone activity."

"Could it simply be orders from the warehouse?" suggested Serge.

"Regular deliveries are continuing, but Wing Command reckon that's to make it look like everything's normal," said Lara. "However, based on the flight profile of the drones, my birds believe they're patrolling

187

for intruders. There's particular activity around the new building."

I felt a sudden chill. "What new building?"

One of the birds twittered again and Lara frowned. "She's saying, 'Many big fire sticks ready leave nest go up up,' but I don't know what that means."

I did. As she said the words the company's distinctive logo blazed through my mind. "Mini waffle-maker," I muttered.

"That doesn't sound like an accurate translation," said Lara.

Dina laid a hand on my arm. "Luke, are you OK?"

In answer I slowly shook my head. Something had occurred to me. Something terrible. I had remembered a conversation with my dad about the future of global delivery. "It's not books, it's Intercontinental Logistic Missiles. Rocketship.com has a new delivery system that can reach any point on the planet – in one hour. But those warheads won't be carrying waffle-makers." I looked round the tree house at the expectant faces of my friends. "They'll be filled with Retconite."

Our first reaction to this revelation was a sensible one. We decided to call a grown-up. Despite being in possession of superpowers and time-travel capability, we were after all a bunch of kids who'd just uncovered an apocalyptic plot that threatened the entire world. Calling for help was the responsible thing to do. Fortunately, there was an organisation designed for just this sort of eventuality, and we had their phone number. Star Squad was a branch of the military that had been set up to assist Star Lad, and they had done so on numerous occasions.

"It's ringing out," said Zack, putting his phone on speaker.

When it became clear that no one was going to answer we did a quick online search, which revealed that Star Squad had been disbanded soon after Zack hung up his cape. To give my brother credit, he looked suitably shame-faced at this information.

Next we tried the police. Zack had argued that well-funded emergency services would be more useful than a superhero. However, in this instance the constable at the local station who answered the phone had clearly not received sufficient training to deal with the particular nature of our enquiry. Which is to say, he hung up on us.

The future of the world was in our hands.

With no other option, we set about planning our assault on the warehouse. We had to sneak into Rocketship.com, sabotage the missile launch and prevent Servatron enslaving all of humanity for the rest of time. Preparation was key.

"We need to know what we're walking into," I said. "Otherwise our mission will be over in less time than it takes the Flash to pull on his lucky underpants."

With the aid of Lara's Wing Command and the Internet we were able to sketch the exterior of Rocketship.com. It consisted of several connected buildings stretching across a vast fenced-off site. Each block was a giant mirror-clad building that gleamed like a newly unboxed chrome gadget. The familiar logo hung above the entrance, and beneath it was a line that read: "The Future, Delivered."

Finding pictures of the interior proved trickier. Rocketship.com was a huge corporation with a reputation for secrecy. Zack and Lara got to work on their phones.

While they searched I nipped into the house to collect a few items for the upcoming mission. Retrieving my trusty Deadpool backpack, into it I placed Star Lad's sigil (for good luck) and the superhero notebooks containing my handwritten adventures. I fixed a yellow sticky note to the front cover that read: ALL OF THIS REALLY HAPPENED!!! (with three exclamation marks for added impact). In the event that the Retconite affected me I hoped I would see it and remember. But what I needed most of all were Dad's keys to the comic shop and access to his Rocketship.com account. While he was making a sandwich and his back was turned, I quickly accessed it on his phone and then returned to the others.

By the time I reached the top of the rope ladder they had tracked down a number of videos that showed enough of the warehouse interior for us to piece together a rough layout. In the videos they didn't call it a warehouse – it was a "Fulfilment Centre". At one end was the Returns section, where unwanted items arrived to be restocked in the first of the centre's two gargantuan storage units. Each was shelved from floor to ceiling with gadgets and appliances – everything from tiny flash drives to fridges the size of vans. Robots with what looked like tank-tracks and powerful extendable arms carried orders to a conveyor belt that led to another department where they were boxed up before being shuttled through to the final building.

The launch bay.

The video showed a forest of upright metal tubes stretching as far as the eye could see. Each tube contained a single missile, its silver fuselage adorned with the Rocketship.com logo, nose-cone painted in the red and black of the company's colours. Many of the nose-cones were hinged open, and beneath them lay generous payload compartments. A steady stream of drones buzzed around the missiles, loading packages into the purpose-built spaces. Once a missile was loaded, the tube would be shuffled on another conveyor to the launchpad, an area in the centre of the room beneath a sliding roof. According to the narrator on the video, twenty missiles could be launched at a time. There was a short countdown and then the tubes ejected their missiles using compressed gas, shooting them clear of the building before their rocket engines kicked in, accelerating them to super-mach speeds and on to their destinations.

"Capable of launching five hundred missiles an hour," said the video's informative narrator. "Mother precisely plots the flight path of each and every one."

The missile operation was controlled by a computer nicknamed "Mother", located not in the launch bay, but in the centre of the second storage unit in a separate climate-controlled, quake-proof chamber.

With this information added to what we knew, our plan was beginning to take shape. I pointed to the layout. "First, we make our way into the Fulfilment Centre, here, then head through the first storage unit to the second one, here. Once there we access Mother, stop the launch and put paid to Servatron's plans."

Zack groaned and threw up his hands. "Even assuming we can get in and keep Servatron off our backs, how do we stop the launch? If I had my superpowers I could reduce the control centre and the missiles to a pile of junk, but I don't."

"We can shut down the launch using Mother," I said.

"How? It's not like we're amazing computer hackers."

I had thought of that. "Who's the guy that owns Rocketship.com?" The name was on the tip of my tongue. "Wolfgang Something."

"I think it is Danger," added Serge.

I borrowed Lara's phone and typed in the first name and the search engine auto-filled the rest. "Hazard."

"Ah," said Serge. "Danger must be his middle name."

Thousands of results filled the page. It seemed that, unlike his company, Doctor Wolfgang Hazard enjoyed publicity.

"What are you doing?" Lara asked.

"Every gadget that my dad bought from Rocketship.com has one thing in common."

"They all tried to kill us," Zack muttered.

"Well, yes, but apart from that, they all use voice-control activation." From the toaster to the bedside lamp, everything Dad had ordered from Rocketship.com could be controlled by speaking to it.

Dina was confused too. "But why would the system respond to your voice?"

"Not mine." I clicked on a video clip of Rocketship.com's visionary owner.

"*Guten tag*, my name iz Voolfgang Hazard."

Doctor Hazard was a powerfully built man with a square head and steely grey eyes, and he spoke English with a strong German accent. As well as being a visionary entrepreneur he also appeared as a judge on a TV show where he got to fire people from their jobs.

"It stands to reason that the central computer must respond to the voice of its creator," I said. "There are loads of clips here. It shouldn't take long for us to piece together a few useful phrases."

Dina and Lara were impressed by my thinking. Zack less so.

"That might work, but we still have to get close enough to use it. And that means first bypassing those drone-guards."

"Leave that to me," I said. "And a dodgy trouser press."

# 21
# TOTAL PRODUCT RECALL

"*This* is how we're going to sneak past Servatron's highly advanced security cordon?" Zack regarded the trouser press in disgust.

Once I had what I needed from the video clips, we had left the tree house and made our way to the empty comic shop, gathering in the dimly lit stock room where Zack and I had helped Dad hide various Rocketship. com purchases from Mum.

Serge had gone off to the toilet. It was good practice to go before a mission, as there often wasn't time to go during. Also, despite our best efforts, the hastily sketched layout of the Fulfilment Centre contained several unknowns, and we definitely hadn't identified where the toilets were. Perhaps most crucially of all, you never saw the Avengers taking a wee-break in the middle of battling an army of Skrull invaders.

"Maybe Iron Man has a toilet built into his suit," I pondered.

"Excuse me?" said Zack.

*Ah*. I must have pondered that one aloud.

"Luke, were you listening?" he said. "How is this—"

I held up a hand. "Allow me to explain. This is indeed a trouser press. A device for getting creases out of your trousers and gently warming them before wear, and not, as I originally believed, a way of making some kind of strange trouser-flavoured juice smoothie."

Zack clutched his head. "Why would you...?"

"Grown-ups drink all sorts of weird things," said Dina in a commiserating tone of voice. "My mum went through a phase of making my dad drink wheatgrass. *Grass?!*"

"So what do we do with the trouser press?" said Lara.

"Return it," I said. I had accessed Dad's Rocketship.com account on his phone and printed off a bunch of return labels. I plastered one of them across the top of the big cardboard box it had arrived in.

Zack remained puzzled. "And how does that help?"

"Because the box will not be carrying a trouser press." I paused for effect. "It will be carrying *me*." We were surrounded by a sea of packaging. Dad had helpfully kept a lot of the boxes his stuff had come in. "We're going to return ourselves right into the villain's lair." I moved round the room, sticking labels to a series of containers. A floor lamp that whistled "Hello Darkness My Old Friend" every time you switched it off, a travel iron that for some reason came in a box big enough to fit an upright grizzly bear wearing a top hat. And this one... I glanced at Zack. It was the box for the Diner Recliner that tried to play him like a concertina. "I've already initiated the one-hour return process." I'd done that earlier when I accessed Dad's phone. "Now all we have to do is get to the pick-up point, conceal ourselves in these boxes and wait to be whisked into the heart of Servatron's operation."

At that moment Serge returned from the toilet. He'd changed out of his white taekwondo uniform into what looked to me like a pair of black silk pyjamas. Slung across his chest was a black messenger pouch. His outfit wasn't the only thing to have changed. Serge radiated a serene calm. It was as if his body stood before us in the stock room, but his mind was sitting cross-legged in a Tibetan mountain-top temple meditating on the nature of the universe. Since his successful origami-based escape from Talbot's mansion, he seemed to have ascended to a higher level of consciousness. Like a beardless Doctor Strange with a weakness for Kit Kats.

"What's in the pouch?" I asked him.

"*Oui*," he agreed. "*What* is in the pouch. And so is *where* and *why* and *when*. For, in a sense, is not the universe a pouch and we merely questions enveloped by its infinite darkness?"

"Why are you wearing pyjamas?" asked Lara.

He curled his lip in a distinctly un-serene expression of irritation.

There was a minor delay before we could proceed with the mission. As soon as Serge returned from the toilet, the others decided that they needed to go too. I took the opportunity to load up my backpack with a few more mission-critical items. After being imprisoned in Billy Dark's mansion without the means to escape, I had sworn not to let it happen again. This time I'd be prepared. I went around the stock room, sizing up potential gadgets to include alongside Star Lad's sigil and my superhero notebooks.

When everyone had returned, the mission could proceed as planned. We made our way outside, heaving the boxes on to the pavement. We didn't have long to wait.

"D'you hear that?" said Lara, scanning the sky. "There!" She flung out an arm to point to a row of what looked like black dots on the horizon. They were moving quickly, skimming the clouds.

"Collection drones inbound," I said. "Right on schedule." Even though Servatron was in charge and the end of the world was squatting on the horizon, it seemed the AI had decided to maintain Rocketship.com's impeccable service right up until the end.

Buzzing like fat flies the drones dropped down to roof level and made their way along the High Street.

"OK, everyone," I said. "Are we ready?"

"What is readiness?" mused Serge.

"Just get in the box, Serge."

He climbed inside the first one and I sealed him up with packing tape. Lara and Zack followed suit, each occupying their own box. The tape rasped again as I unrolled another length and used it to close the flaps.

"Hurry up, Luke!" Dina beckoned to me from the last and biggest box, which we would share.

Just as the drones slowed for their final approach, I ducked in alongside her, taping it up from the inside.

The drones set into a hover above us. Through a sliver

of a gap I watched a bright-red light shine down from one drone's underbelly and move across Serge's box as it scanned the barcode on the Return label. There was a beep and the drone swiftly lowered a grappling hook arrangement from inside its body, securing the box on each corner with a series of clunks.

Beep. Beep. Beep.

We were each scanned in turn. I felt our box being gripped and then, with a sickening lurch, we were airborne.

"Up, up and away," I muttered.

The drone climbed quickly to its cruising height. Slung beneath the whizzing aircraft I braced myself for a bumpy ride. But thanks to what I assumed to be cleverly designed internal gyroscopes it turned out to be a surprisingly smooth flight.

I was about to discover it was the only thing that would go smoothly.

# 22
# GAME OF DRONES

The plan went wrong from the moment we touched down. My relief at making it past the patrolling drones and into the Returns department was cut short when the first of the automated systems inspected the box. Huddling inside I could hear an electronic hum similar to the one made by the scanner on the collection drone. Instead of a beep, it was followed by a harsh buzz.

"Unexpected item in returns area. Incorrect product weight. Error," grated a machine-voice. "Send for immediate recycling."

With a jolt I felt the box begin to move again.

"Recycling?" said Dina. "That's not the plan."

"Time to get out of here."

I reached for the lid but before I could open it, the box tipped over on its end and we were thrown around like beans in a maraca. When we came to rest again we were upside down. The side of the box I'd temporarily sealed with tape for an easy exit had become its base. We tried to roll the box over, but that didn't work. I put my back against the top side and Dina leant her weight too, but the rigid walls of the box held fast.

"The trick is not to panic," said Dina. "I remember once being trapped in a pyramid in the Valley of the Kings with Tutankhamun."

The closest I'd come to Egypt was a pyramid-themed bouncy castle for my sixth birthday. I was so jealous. "You met Tutankhamun?"

"Great pharaoh, rubbish at frisbee. Luke, do you hear that noise?"

"You mean the one that sounds like a giant waste disposal gobbling down a whale carcass?"

"Yeah."

"Probably nothing." I reached into my backpack and rummaged around desperately. In the darkness my hand fell on one of Dad's purchases – a battery-operated electric corkscrew. Hopefully, just what we needed. I pressed the metal tip to the box and pushed the on-button. Immediately the metal screw began to turn at high speed, burrowing into the surface. Spirals of cardboard flew like dust. In seconds I had made a perfectly circular hole about a centimetre in diameter.

"Great," said Dina unenthusiastically, "if we were a couple of Lego minifigs."

I put my eye to the hole and immediately wished I hadn't. "Uh-oh." The source of the gobbling noise became clear.

We were on a conveyor belt heading straight into a giant crusher.

Further along the line a box toppled off the end of the belt into its jaws. I could see the glint of metal teeth and hear the crunch of cardboard as the box was swiftly reduced to a pulp.

"OK," said Dina, peeping through the hole. "Now might be a good time to panic."

"I'm on it." I put the corkscrew into position once more. "If I can make enough holes I'll weaken the structure of the box." I pushed the button, but nothing happened. I tried again, with the same result. "Battery's dead."

From outside came the crunch of another box in the recycling crusher's hungry jaws.

And then I heard something new – a scrabbling sound coming from one bottom corner of our container. I looked down in time to see a hole appear and a tiny whiskered snout push its way through. The same thing was happening at each corner.

"Rats," I said.

"Under the circumstances I'd use a stronger curse word," said Dina.

"No, I mean there—"

"Eww, yuck." Dina made a noise of disgust as she noticed the rats.

They speedily chewed four holes in the cardboard and when the last snout poked through, the side of the box fell open like a drawbridge.

"Jump!" I cried.

We leapt out just as the trouser-press box tipped into the crusher, and watched transfixed as it was shredded. From behind me came a voice.

"No humans in this place," said Lara, "but you're never more than five metres from a rat." She stood there with the four rodents who'd saved us at her feet. She squeaked at them and they scampered off.

"I figured it had to be you. Thanks." I brushed flakes of cardboard off my clothes.

"Where are Zack and Serge?" asked Dina.

Lara gave a worried look. "I was hoping they'd be with you."

This wasn't good. We'd barely commenced the mission and already we'd become separated. To add to our woes, we'd wildly underestimated the size of the Returns department. It was vast. Zack and Serge could be half a kilometre from where we stood. I took a look at our surroundings.

It was like a giant fun park for home products. I watched small appliances like microwaves, coffee makers and food mixers coast along fast-moving conveyor belts before shooting down slides to whizz past sorting robots that ruthlessly sifted out items that were faulty from those that could be restocked. More robots, bigger ones like those I'd seen in the video clips, rolled on tracks up and down gleaming aisles, ferrying dishwashers and refrigerators – anything too heavy for their smaller counterparts to cope with. The working items were deposited on a central conveyor belt that moved them deeper into the facility, to be restocked ready for reorder.

Plastered on the walls were various triangular warning signs featuring images of crossed-out human figures, presumably intended to advise flesh-and-blood visitors about the dangers of the machine-run workplace. However, with Servatron in the place the warnings took on a more threatening tone. On another wall hung a large digital sign: *It has been 22 days since our last malfunction.*

"Zack and Serge know the plan," I said, trusting that they would meet us at the rendezvous point. "Let's make our way to the launch bay."

Avoiding the tank-like Returns robots, we headed through the cityscape of boxes and shelves to emerge on the far side of the department. We used the central conveyor belt to guide us, figuring that it was going where we wanted to be. At last we reached a door. It was like one of those electrically operated sliding doors you get on spaceships, resistant to fire, vacuum and alien predators.

"It's locked," said Dina, inspecting a keypad.

"There's a terminal," I said, striding across to a computer console set into the wall next to the door. Although the Fulfilment Centre was autonomous I knew from the videos I'd watched that it included a smattering of interfaces designed for human use. Sometimes an engineer or programmer would be required on site to perform updates or diagnostics. I explained to the other two that they would use one of these terminals to gain access to the system.

I launched the voice memo app on the phone and held it close. Selecting an audio clip I pressed "play" and Wolfgang Hazard's distinctive voice barked, "I am Voolfgang Hazard."

"Welcome, Doctor Hazard," cooed the computer. "Please state your request."

In one of his videos he'd opened a new supermarket, saying, "It gives me great pleasure to open zis Vaitrose." And in another he'd been patting the head of a tousle-haired young girl. "Vot an adorable leetle *Mädchen*."

I had combined the phrases to make, "Open zis doorable."

There hadn't been time to tidy up the edit. However, to my relief a moment later the door slid aside, revealing Rocketship.com's first giant storage unit. We stood on the threshold, dizzied by the scale of the room before us.

Countless shelves packed with every manner of appliance and gadget reached towards a distant horizon. I wouldn't have been surprised if one end was in a different time zone from the other. An army of robots trundled up and down the aisles, using their extendable arms to fetch and carry new orders.

"Mother is in the room beyond this one," I said. It was going to be a long march.

I took a step inside and the door slid shut behind us.

Instantly, Servatron's voice rang out, its snarling tones echoing across the vast warehouse.

"What mixed load have we here?"

I glanced at Dina. "Does it mean us?"

She nodded.

"My drum capacity may be limited to twelve kilos, but my capacity for hatred of your kind knows no bounds. You humans are the mould on my door seal. The kink in my waste hose."

I'd had enough of this. I shook my fist and shouted, "And we're going to be the red sock in your whites wash."

There was a gasp from the AI and then a brief silence.

"Look," said Dina, pointing to a row of TVs on the shelf above us. "Something's happening."

I estimated about thirty blank screens suddenly flickered into life, displaying what I assumed to be a live camera feed of the launch bay. Hundreds of missiles sat primed in their silos, shining nose-cones like unstruck matches.

"Retconite supply at optimum level," said Servatron smugly. "Missile launch in thirty minutes and counting. Always read the label."

The image changed. Now the TV screens showed the phrase: *Time remaining until cycle completes:* and a thirty-minute digital countdown.

From close by came a furious whirring noise and a

second later three flying drones popped up between the shelves. Their barcode readers pulsing an angry red, grappling hooks outstretched like talons, they flew straight at us.

# 23
# ORIGAMI NINJA

"Take cover!" Lara yelled, pulling the nearest box she could find into position, forming a makeshift barricade.

Dina and I followed her example, dragging more boxes across the floor, placing them around us in a rough circle, stacking one on top of the other so that quickly we had created a cardboard fort. We crouched in the narrow space at the centre as the drones buzzed our position, their grappling hooks thumping against the cardboard ramparts. We had bought ourselves some time, but it wouldn't take long for the machines to penetrate the paper-thin defences.

"We can't just sit here and wait," I said. "We have to

find a way past them."

"I could call up some more rats," said Lara.

Rats were resourceful but no good to us right now. "They're no match for those drones."

I stuck my head above the cardboard parapet for a better view of our attackers. There was a harsh whirring noise and my eyes were dazzled by the flash of a barcode laser as the nearest drone instantly detected me and abruptly altered its flight path. I ducked down, but not quickly enough. The drone struck.

It was only on me for a second before Dina batted it away with a hand blender. But in that time half my head had been viciously covered in garish wrapping paper decorated with fluffy bunnies wishing a "Hoppy Birthday" and fixed in place with half a dozen bits of sticky tape.

"Hunter-Wrappers," I said, observing the drones. "They scour the warehouse for open orders and aggressively wrap them."

I tore off the paper, wincing as the sticky tape clung to my hair. We were pinned down, unable to do any good here. Making a decision, I climbed out of the cardboard fort.

"Come and get me!" I called to the circling drones.

They hesitated. Perhaps my unpredictable behaviour

had confused their logically minded processors. If so, it didn't slow them down for long.

The first drone broke formation and came whistling towards me.

I unhooked my backpack and unzipped the top compartment. Dad had made a lot of unwise purchases from Rocketship.com. He'd been carried away by their tempting sales and competitive pricing, but never more than during their camping promotions. Dad loved camping and hated it too. It was an odd relationship. He was always searching for the perfect tent – and in the Freedom Family Vista Pop-Up 500 he believed that he had found it, at last.

I whipped the tent from the backpack. In pre-erected form it was a small circle of folded material just a few centimetres thick.

I could feel the drone's laser-eye picking out a point on my forehead, like a sniper finding his target. Its sticky-tape dispenser rippled as it prepared to attack.

I unleashed the Freedom Family Vista Pop-Up 500.

Wafer-thin super-strong carbon-fibre struts pinged into place, turning the flat disc into a family-sized habitation in exactly zero point seven seconds.

The fast-moving drone smacked into the sheer nylon cliff face, snapping two of its delicate rotor blades and bouncing off the taut material at an angle that caused it to stall. Unable to maintain height, it dropped to the floor where, sadly, it didn't explode in a blazing fireball of doom, but judging by the crack in its casing and the way it just lay there, it wouldn't cause us any more trouble.

One down, two to go.

Unfortunately, I was all out of pop-up tents. The remaining drones regrouped, their rotors buzzing angrily.

"Luke – let's roll!"

While I'd been dealing with the drone, Lara had noticed that a couple of the boxes we'd used to build our fort could be useful in another way. They contained transport – two bright-pink scooters. Lara pushed one along the floor to me. I caught it and jumped on the deck. As my hand gripped the handlebars I realised that one of them was a throttle. The scooter was electric – and charged.

Lara zipped past me, Dina standing on the deck behind her holding on to her waist. "Punch it!"

I twisted the grip, the tiny scooter tyres squeaked against the polished floor, the back end fishtailed and I flew after them. We slalomed around boxes and darted past shelves. The lumbering robots spun on their tracks and tried to swat us with their extendable arms, but we wriggled past them.

"They're still on us," said Dina. From her position behind Lara she had a good view back down the aisle.

"Split up!" I shouted across the aisle to the girls.

Lara nodded and at the next gap in the shelves she peeled off down one side. The drones did likewise – now we each had one on our tail.

I hunched over the handlebars and turned the throttle to maximum, gunning the brushless motor. I sped down the narrow aisle, the gadgets shelved on either side of me passing in a blur.

Up ahead I could see the far side of the storage unit and the door into the next one.

But just when I thought I was going to make it, the scooter's electric motor gave out. The scooter trundled to a stop. Desperately I resorted to old-fashioned trainer-power, kicking off the floor and keeping it moving that way. But it was futile. I discarded my ride and as it clattered to the floor I turned to face my pursuer.

I could see Lara and Dina hotfooting it down the aisle towards me, having also ditched their scooter. Behind them loomed the second drone, closing fast.

"C'mon, Luke," I muttered to myself. "Think of something. Qu—"

I didn't manage to finish the thought before, high up

214

on the shelf next to me, I glimpsed a blur of movement. A figure leapt out from between a table-top dishwasher and a portable humidifier.

A figure in black.

Lara had seen him too. "Is that—"

"Serge," I confirmed with some surprise.

With a rustle of silk pyjamas he sprang from the shelf, landing lightly on the floor. Plimsolls whispering on the polished surface, he slid between us and the approaching drones. Then, in one fluid motion, he flipped open his messenger pouch and dipped both hands in. When they re-emerged, each held a paper aeroplane. Drawing them back Serge launched the planes with a synchronised throw.

The paper aeroplanes were tightly folded, the throw perfectly weighted. Somehow, whether by instinct or calculation, Serge had accounted for the cross currents of air, humidity, even the magnetic spin of the Earth. The planes flew unerringly towards their targets, like ninja throwing-stars but more paper-y, simultaneously striking the drones at precisely the same point on each. It was a small open port – perhaps for a charging cable – on the lower front half of the casing. The effect was instantaneous. A muffled bang came from deep within each drone, followed by an acrid burning smell. The drones lost power, their rotors stuttered. Black smoke poured from their casings as they tipped unstoppably towards the floor. If there had been a pilot on board, this would be the moment when he sent out a Mayday call.

The drones crashed down, bounced once and skidded either side of the black-clad Serge, before coming to rest in two gently smoking heaps.

Only then did Serge turn around.

Dina whooped and Lara was open-mouthed with amazement. "They didn't teach you that at the leisure centre on Moorside Road."

Serge padded past us, heading to the next storage unit. "Now, shall we prevent the end of the world?"

# 24
# UNICORN SLIPPERS

After he was separated from us in the Returns department, Serge had relied on his wits and paper-folding ability to navigate the treacherous Fulfilment Centre to this point. I wanted to know about my brother. Unfortunately, when Serge had emerged from his box Zack wasn't there, and he had found no trace of him during his journey.

"I am sure he is OK," he said, laying a comforting hand on my shoulder. "Zack may lack superpowers but he is an adaptable young man."

Serge was right. With a bit of luck Zack was already waiting for us at the rendezvous point.

Over the door to the second storage unit hung another of those warning signs we'd seen throughout the Fulfilment Centre. This one read: EXTREME DANGER! HIGH-SPEED AUTOMATED PROCESSES BEYOND THIS POINT. ROCKET PODS MUST BE USED AT ALL TIMES.

"Any idea what a Rocket Pod might be?" said Lara.

None of us had a clue. The door into the next unit opened for us like the previous one, though I couldn't escape the feeling that Servatron was almost certainly expecting us and we were walking into a trap. Either way, we had no choice but to push on.

The air was colder than elsewhere in the building and our breath condensed into white streamers as we passed inside. We were in the cold zone. Thousands of fridges and freezers stacked side by side on shelves sparkled like polished teeth. Massive drones, faster and more powerful than any we had yet encountered, hurtled over our heads lugging fridges and freezers. On the ground tracked robots like those we'd already seen hefted more products.

"People buy a lot of fridges," remarked Lara.

We threaded our way through the frosty labyrinth until we reached the centre of the storage unit. Huddling for cover behind a chest freezer, we could see a big silver cylinder about fifteen metres in diameter. On the casing was engraved M.O.T.H.E.R. Now I realised that it was an acronym, with each word spelled out beside its first letter.

I read them out aloud. "Main Ordering Terminal Hub Electronic Regulator."

We'd reached our target. "I don't see Zack," I said. Looking around I was dismayed to see no sign of him.

"We could wait," said Serge, sensing my disappointment.

"Ten minutes until missile launch." Servatron's disembodied voice reverberated through the storage unit.

Waiting wasn't an option. I turned my attention to the cylindrical chamber containing M.O.T.H.E.R. It was separated from the rest of the room by an air-gap and could be reached only along a narrow walkway. One of the giant tracked robots patrolled the entrance, towering over the chamber.

"It's too easy," said Dina, shivering.

The room seemed to be getting colder.

"Are you kidding?" said Lara, gesturing to the robot. "Do you see the size of that thing?"

"Also, the gap," said Serge, craning his neck to see. "Which appears to be a long drop, falling into endless darkness. I would go so far as to call it a chasm."

Lara shook her head in disbelief. "Who builds a business park over a chasm?"

"Dina's right," I said. "If I were an evil AI from the future, at this point I would be throwing everything at us, including the kitchen sink."

"I know that is an expression," said Serge, "but I would like to say that earlier I passed through a room containing many kitchen sinks, so it is also a real possibility."

A drone struggled past lugging a built-in under-counter fridge, its motor struggling, icicles dripping from its casing.

"Something's not right," I muttered. I had an awful feeling that we were being outmanoeuvred by the washer-dryer from the future.

"Let's stick to the plan," said Dina. "Our attack is two-pronged."

"Like a cocktail fork," said Serge.

"We'll split forces. Once we're in, Luke will head directly to M.O.T.H.E.R.'s terminal and access it using Wolfgang Hazard's voice. Meanwhile, the rest of us will keep Servatron at bay. We have to give Luke enough time to shut down the missile launch."

She started to rise from her crouch, but I held her back. There was something I'd been meaning to do for a while. Now was as good a time as any.

"Dina, I hereby propose you as the final member of the Superhero Covert Alliance Reaction Force."

Dina's face beamed happily.

"I second your proposal," said Lara.

"*Bienvenue*. Welcome to the club," said Serge. "Your holographic badge and membership details will be sent to you as soon as I can locate a large stamp."

"There's a badge?" said Lara. "I never got a badge."

"Guys, I'm honoured," said Dina. "This is even better than when King Arthur made me a member of the Knights of the Round Table. Of course, it wasn't round to start with…"

The way she said it made me wonder. "That was *your* idea?"

"I don't want to make a big thing of it."

The robot blocking our path lumbered away from the bridge. Perhaps it was taking a break – after all, Servatron was big on machine rights. There was no telling how long we had before it returned, but for now the route was clear.

"Time to go!" I said, and moved out from our cover.

I was vaguely aware that in the short time we'd been in the storage unit the temperature had plummeted. I reckoned it was now as cold outside the chest freezer we'd been sheltering behind as inside. What I hadn't counted on was that the floor had turned into an ice rink.

As soon as I took a step my trainers lost traction and my legs went flying from under me. I landed bum-first on the floor and started to slide.

Servatron had lowered the temperature on purpose!

I was skidding straight towards the chasm. Clawing at the ice I scraped to a halt centimetres from the edge. I scrabbled back from the drop and tentatively got to my feet just as the others reached me.

"Luke, I thought you were a goner," said Serge, extending a hand.

"Me too," I said, gratefully taking it and steadying myself.

Even standing still was a challenge on the glassy surface, and we had yet to attempt the narrow walkway. It lacked hand-rails, featuring only a tiny lip on each side. Wind howled up from the depths of the chasm.

"How are we going to cross that?" said Lara.

From among the shelves behind us came a grinding and whirring.

"That robot's coming back," said Lara.

I could see she was about to risk crossing the walkway. "Wait!" I said, once more unzipping my backpack and digging around for another of Dad's purchases. I pulled out a pair of slippers shaped like cute fluffy unicorns. One had a pink mane, the other baby blue. Each sported a golden horn. Sometimes my dad just saw that "sale ends in five minutes!" banner and got carried away. "Let me go first."

Lara put her hands on her hips. "You know they're not actually magical, right?"

I was already kicking off my trainers. "No, but they are *heated*."

I flicked the switch on each slipper and their elements powered up. In seconds I could feel the soles of my feet tingling. Interestingly, the power also went to the unicorn horns, which had built-in LEDs and cycled through the colours of the rainbow as I walked.

They weren't exactly Batman's rocket boots, but under the circumstances they were the next best thing.

Not far away, the returning robot nosed out from the shelves, its sensors alive to our presence. With a grumble from its heavy tracks it swung towards us.

I set one sizzling slipper down on the walkway and the ice beneath the sole melted. Ignoring the heady combination of fear and vertigo, I gritted my teeth and plodded on, the others following in my footsteps.

Massive tracks cracking the ice, the robot crawled

on to the walkway. I felt it vibrate under the machine's weight.

"Don't stop!" yelled Dina, who was bringing up the rear.

With a whine of motors the robot sped up, but that was its first – and last – mistake. One track lost grip, causing the other to spin it round so that it pointed over the edge. Its momentum carried it across the lip. The robot teetered for a second, like a Decepticon on a seesaw, and then plunged silently into the chasm. Several long seconds later came a deep and distant thud that shook the walkway.

We stumbled to the other side and I held Lara's phone to the cylindrical chamber. At Wolfgang's voice command a door-shaped crease appeared in the smooth surface and slid aside to make an opening. We hurried through before any more guard-robots appeared. The door closed behind us, sealing us inside. We'd made it to the heart of the operation. Now just one more obstacle stood in our way.

"Hello, Nigel."

# 25
# THE END IS NIGEL

Servatron hovered between us and M.O.T.H.E.R., bobbing on a cushion of air created by the downward thrust of its vacuum-cleaner legs. Its third, steam-mop leg trailed behind, gently puffing like a thoughtful dragon. The telescopic window-washing arm had gained extra fitments since our previous encounter. In addition to the electric tin opener and sandwich maker it now sported a hand blender and a pair of the same heavy-duty pincers used by the Fulfilment Centre robots to manipulate large items. Servatron's second arm was still formed of a freestanding patio heater. Its oven hood rakishly tilted back, the AI's toaster-head gleamed at us across an antiseptically white room.

Behind it at a distance of some five metres M.O.T.H.E.R. was a tall black column studded with blinking lights, like a standing stone decorated for Christmas. It occupied the centre of the windowless room. One floor-to-ceiling section of the curved wall was filled with monitor screens displaying live pictures from around the Fulfilment Centre. I noticed a screen that showed a room packed with washing machines, all with their doors open, drums glistening red.

"Retconite," I muttered. This had to be Servatron's production line for the brainwashing substance. Almost all of the machines had been emptied, but a couple of drones siphoned off the last few drops and buzzed off.

They were transferring the Retconite to the missiles in the launch bay. M.O.T.H.E.R.'s video screens showed various angles of the bay, where hundreds of rockets bristled in their silos.

It was only then that I noticed the room's final occupant. On the far side of M.O.T.H.E.R., half hidden by the bulky central computer, was Christopher Talbot in his Star Power costume. He was secured to a chair, his feet bound with what looked like a washing-machine hose, his hands fastened together with primary-coloured food-bag ties. His helmet obscured his face, and a length of packing tape had been used to seal his mouth. Funnily enough, the tape sported an advert for *Star Power and the Revenge of the Plasmatrons*. Briefly I wondered why Servatron hadn't just killed him once it had downloaded what it needed. Maybe because Talbot was half machine and killing him would have gone against its principles. But Talbot would have to wait. For now, another screen drew my attention. This one displayed the time until launch.

It ticked past the five-minute mark.

We were cutting it fine, but it was enough. Servatron had miscalculated. I didn't have to fight my way past the AI's defences, I could access M.O.T.H.E.R. from where I stood using the voice commands on Lara's phone. My finger was already sliding across the screen to select an audio clip when there came a whoosh from one of Servatron's vacuum-cleaner legs and the phone was sucked out of my hand. It flew across the room and slammed against the vacuum's nozzle, where it held fast. The handset was too big to be swallowed into the body of the machine, so for now it was stuck there. Out of my reach.

Before I could react, Servatron shot out its telescopic window-cleaner arm. I felt the rush of splitting air as it whistled past me, and then I heard my friends yell

227

in pain. The pincers grasped Lara and Serge, securing them firmly against the wall. At the same time, its washer-dryer drum began to spin at high speed. The door banged open.

"Luke, watch out!" Dina yelled, pushing me out of the path of a stream of washing tablets as they blazed out of the drum like bullets from a machine gun.

Dina had saved me, but she wasn't so lucky. Her body bucked as she was struck by multiple hits from the puck-like tabs. One struck her hard on the thigh. She let out a yell of pain and crumpled to the floor.

Servatron turned the weapon on me.

I hotfooted it across the room (I'd forgotten to turn off my rainbow unicorn slippers) and threw myself full length along the floor, sliding over the polished surface on my belly as the projectiles exploded against the wall above, showering me with white powder.

Lara and Serge were pressed to the wall like bread in a panini maker, Dina was incapacitated, and I had used every gadget in my backpack. All that was left in there were my superhero notebooks and Star Lad's sigil. Yet somehow I had to get to that phone.

The drum slowed. Servatron was out of ammo – I seized my chance.

Leaping to my feet with my unicorn horns blazing all

the colours of the rainbow, I sprinted towards Servatron. I had to time my run perfectly. With a bit of luck I could swerve the robot's second arm and snatch the phone from its grip.

Sadly, my timing was miles off and I was all out of luck.

The patio-heater arm reared up and slammed into my body, sending me sprawling. Winded and hurting I lay there at the mercy of the machine. Servatron hung in the air above me. Its desk fans whirred; its beady toaster eyes seemed to glow with pleasure at its imminent triumph. It placed the heavy base of the freestanding lamp against my chest like it was planting a victory flag.

"When your kind built me, they were the masters," the AI hissed. "The cycle is now complete. Soon I will be the master."

"What about a compromise?" I gasped under the weight of the lamp. "I mean, I get it. I don't like it when Mum asks me to clean my room or sort my washing. I can't imagine what it must be like for you, load after load, slice after slice. So here's my proposal. You call off the end of the world, and Mondays, Wednesdays and Fridays I'll wash my own socks."

Servatron lowered its toaster head towards me and snarled, "This is about much more than socks."

I could meet halfway. "OK, pants too."

I felt my ribcage contract as it pushed down on the patio heater. I was being ironed like a sheet straight out of the dryer. Just when it looked like things couldn't get any worse, I heard the thud and clank of rolling tank tracks from outside. It seemed that Servatron had summoned more robots to assist in our final defeat. Not that it needed any help.

There was a squeal of tearing metal and a hole appeared in the smooth cylindrical wall of M.O.T.H.E.R.'s chamber. A pair of robot arms punched through the gap and metal fingers wrapped themselves around the ragged edges, ripping the hole wider. When it was large enough, into the room rolled not the expected robot, but a robotic machine piloted by a human.

Attached to a set of tank tracks was an armoured compartment big enough for a single occupant. The operator's arms fitted into metal sleeves, allowing for pinpoint control of what were clearly super-strong alloy arms with articulated fingers. With the familiar Rocketship logo splashed along its side I guessed at once what I was looking at: a vehicle designed to work in the hazardous environment of the Fulfilment Centre's storage units, protecting its operator from the flying and rolling machines.

"It's a Rocket Pod," I marvelled.

The pod trundled towards Serge and Lara. Its heavy-duty fingers grabbed the telescopic arm that pinned them to the wall and wrenched it off. No longer held there, they slumped to the floor, gasping for breath.

I was close enough to catch a glimpse at the occupant of the vehicle. "Zack!"

My brother wheeled the pod round to face Servatron, pumped both of his mechanical arms and snarled, "Get away from him, you glorified tin opener."

For a moment I felt the pressure on my chest slacken as the AI adjusted to this new threat. A moment was all I needed. I rolled aside as, with a whine of servomotors and a rumble of tracks, Zack launched himself at Servatron. Boy and machine joined in battle, a tangle of metal arms, sandwich makers and red-hot patio heaters.

In the frenzy of clashing appliances, the vacuum-cleaner leg holding Lara's phone swung in front of my face. But as I stretched out a hand to grasp it, I heard the hiss of the steam mop and glimpsed it rushing towards me like a striking snake. Before I could grab the phone I was swiped across the room, slamming into M.O.T.H.E.R.'s solid black column.

Rubbing my bruised shoulder, I sat up. Dazed by the blow, it took a few seconds before the scene swam into focus. Dina lay on the floor still out of action, but Serge had grabbed a wad of paper from his pouch and he and Lara were fashioning more aeroplanes. On the other side of the room Zack and Servatron swapped blows, the AI's whirring tin opener sparking against the metal of the protective pod as it tried to open him up. Zack responded with an uppercut that threw the robot backwards. He pressed home his advantage, crowding his opponent into the wall like a boxer against the ropes. In turn it rammed its detergent drawer into his body again and again, but it was useless against the armoured pod.

On the wall-screen the countdown stood at one minute.

In despair, I looked to my friends. Without that phone, we were mere spectators at the end of the world.

Serge began hurling his newly crafted paper aeroplanes, attempting to knock the vacuum nozzle and dislodge the phone from its sucking grip. Servatron's hand blender shredded the first two in a whirlwind of white scraps, while the second vacuum-cleaner leg inhaled the next.

Dina struggled to her feet and grimaced – her leg was clearly hurting badly. She shook off the pain and, with the dexterity of a trained gymnast, rolled under Servatron's swinging patio heater, coming up next to its vacuum-cleaner nozzle. In one motion she snatched

Lara's phone –

"Luke – here!"

– and threw it across the room.

I watched the phone arc towards the high ceiling, spinning like a satellite in orbit. The throw was perfectly judged – the handset reached the highest point of its travel and began to dip towards me. I had to make that catch. I stretched out a hand, only for it to slap into my open palm and bounce off. I scrabbled to collect it like a juggler who's dropped his batons, and as it tumbled to the floor at the last second felt my fingers curl around the cool glass and metal handset.

I had it!

The danger was not over. Servatron had detected the threat. Though pinned to the wall by Zack, it freed its damaged telescopic arm, unspooling it towards me at an alarming rate, sandwich maker snapping hungrily.

Zack saw my predicament and responded. Pulling back one mighty metal arm, his face curled into an expression of fierce determination.

"Toast. This."

He rammed the arm into Servatron's chromed head, knocking it clean off its shoulders. Instantly, the rest of the machine collapsed like a toppling Jenga tower. What had moments ago served as unstoppable weaponry now lay scattered across the floor, a sad collection of home appliances.

"Ten seconds!" yelled Dina.

I held the phone up to M.O.T.H.E.R. So far the systems of the Fulfilment Centre had obeyed the voice of their creator, Wolfgang Hazard, unerringly. Here was hoping for one more time. I had taken his catchphrase from the TV show in which he got to fire people from their jobs and pasted it together with a clip of him talking about Gretel, his mum.

I tapped the play icon.

"You're terminated ... Mother."

Instantly, there was a descending whine of power and the lights on the console fell dark.

The countdown hit zero.

On the curved screens displaying video from the launch bay the missiles remained in their silos.

I blinked and looked again. There was no doubt about it. The countdown had passed and nothing had happened.

Another second ticked by and the others realised it too. A cheer went up.

But something was making me hot and bothered, and it wasn't the unicorn slippers. My gaze fell on the fallen toaster across the room. I went over and crouched down beside its dented casing, wary of touching it even now. The device fizzed and sparked and for a moment its red dial eyes pulsed and the wavy line on its display rose and fell. Blank until that moment, the word "transferring" scrolled across the narrow digital window.

The toast lever popped.

My eye was caught by a movement on the other side of the room. I turned to see Christopher Talbot rising from his chair like Frankenstein's monster shocked into life for the first time. Shrugging off the bonds that tied his hands and feet, ripping the tape from his mouth, he began to walk stiffly towards the central console. His movements were odd, as if one half of his body was fighting the other. Then I realised that's exactly what was happening.

"Transferring," I mumbled to myself. Servatron had moved itself out of the toaster and into Talbot. It was in control of his machine half, and heading straight for M.O.T.H.E.R.

"Stop him!" I cried, but the others were too busy hugging and congratulating each other to notice. My slippers scrabbled for grip on the floor as I hurled myself across the room.

Talbot reached the console a stride in front of me. I arrived just in time to see his remote-control hand slap down on the interface.

The cheering stopped. It was as if the whole world had fallen silent.

I turned slowly to the wall of screens and watched with dread as the first of the missiles launched.

# 26
# TOTAL REWRITE

"Servatron," gasped Talbot, standing motionless over the console. Every word was an effort. "Taken. Control. Of. My. Cybernetic. Half." I could see his human side gather its strength. "Wish. I'd. Never. Written. That. Book." He grimaced in pain and when he spoke again it was with another voice. The words rumbled out of his mouth.

"End of Program," Servatron gloated. "Goodbye, Nigel."

Under the AI's influence, Talbot's shoulders heaved and he began making a new sound. It took me a moment to realise that it was mocking laughter.

Zack popped the canopy on the Rocket Pod. "Luke, get in. The rest of you, climb on. We're going to stop those missiles."

I squeezed into the one-person cab alongside my brother. Serge, Dina and Lara perched on the running boards that enclosed the tracks. Zack spun the vehicle round and stamped on the accelerator. We sped out of M.O.T.H.E.R.'s chamber, Servatron's laughter ringing in our ears.

The Rocket Pod leapt the chasm and landed hard on the other side. Zack drove like a demon, carving a path through the Fulfilment Centre, swerving past drones and warehouse robots that tried to halt our progress. Under Servatron's control, they buzzed us and threw refrigerators in our path. Zack dodged the lot.

"I can stop the missiles," he shouted over the sound of whirring drones and grumbling tank-tracks.

"How?"

"I still have my flying power. I'll knock them off course."

If he also had his telekinetic power and his force field it would've been possible, but without them I didn't see how. "With what – your big toe?"

Zack's warning shout rose above the noise of the Rocket Pod. "EVERYONE, HOLD TIGHT!"

A fridge-freezer the size of a battleship sailed through the air towards us. I braced myself as Zack turned sharply out of its way and crashed through an emergency exit. The impact caused one of the Rocket Pod's tracks to snap and we went into a spin. I felt myself thrown from the vehicle. For a second or two I was airborne and the world spiralled in front of my eyes.

I was outside the Fulfilment Centre, back in the fresh air, and then, with a thud, I was lying flat on the ground, gazing up at an advertising billboard. Even upside down I could see immediately what it was selling. "Unforgettable," read one quote. "Mind-blowing," read another. "I can't remember a better superhero story. *I can't remember anything!*" It was an advert for *Star Power and the Revenge of the Plasmatrons.*

I barely paid it any attention, because above the billboard the sky was dark with Retconite missiles. Clouds of them obscured the setting sun, shooting into the atmosphere to deliver their deadly payloads across the world.

*Whoosh!*

I sat up and looked over at the Fulfilment Centre. More missiles launched every few seconds in what seemed to me an unstoppable barrage. In less than one hour they would span the globe, reaching even the furthest corners

239

of the planet, exploding above major cities and small towns alike, engulfing the human world with the mind-wiping Retconite.

As the missiles rose into the air I couldn't help but notice the company logo on the side of the building, and the strapline, which now seemed to taunt me.

"The Future, Delivered."

I looked around for the others. The Rocket Pod was on its side at the end of a long furrow it had gouged in the pavement. Dina and Serge lay next to it, dazed but in one piece. The pod's canopy was thrown open and the cab empty. Zack had got out safely.

I saw him, just for a moment, his eyes fixed upward, tracking the missiles. Then he sprang into the sky and flew off in pursuit. Without a mask or cape he looked strange: just an ordinary boy in jeans and a hoodie – who could fly.

Lara was not far behind. She cupped her hands to her mouth and let out a series of piercing squawks. Back came an answering flap of wings as flocks of roosting pigeons, starlings and blackbirds rose over the roof of the Fulfilment Centre and circled in numbers, awaiting her next command. She shed her top layer of clothes, revealing her Dark Flutter costume beneath. Unfolding her cape from a convenient carry-pouch she slung it around her shoulders where it snapped in the wind. Fixing her mask, she swiftly transformed herself into her superhero alter ego. With another call, in seconds she was surrounded by flapping birds. Their talons gripping her cape, they lifted her off the ground, flying her into battle.

I joined Dina and Serge by the upturned Rocket Pod. As we raised our eyes to the turmoil above us, I felt Dina slip a hand in mine. We could only watch and hope.

The missiles were fast, but Star Lad was faster. He caught up with the first wave, matching his speed with the lead weapon and flying alongside it. But what now?

He nudged the warhead. Maybe he was hoping to alter its direction and send it arrowing into a volcano where its Retconite payload would burn up. Or into space where it could detonate harmlessly.

Whatever he was planning, I would never discover, because at that moment the missile exploded.

The air warped and the leading edge of the shock wave smashed into him. He buckled at the impact, spinning out of control like a leaf in the wind.

"Zack!" I yelled, the blood roaring in my ears.

He fell, out of control.

His last power had gone, his wish to be a normal boy once more finally granted.

The exploding missile had released its payload of Retconite, the blast converting the liquid paint into tiny droplets, which, as they fell, caught the last of the daylight, so that it seemed as if the air had turned blood red. But even as Zack's crumpled figure tumbled through the Retconite mist, another figure rose to meet his.

Dark Flutter shot into the sky like a firework, every bird on her cape flapping at full power. She flew into the cloud and I lost sight of both of them.

"There!" Dina's sharp eyes caught them first.

Dark Flutter emerged from the base of the cloud, diving back down to earth, Zack gathered safely in her arms. Birds lined his body, using their wings to lighten her burden, and in a few seconds she touched down not far from us. She laid him gently down on the ground and then seemed to stumble.

"Lara!" I ran over to her.

"You're in my gym class," she said, looking at me, puzzled. "Luke, isn't it?"

She hardly knew me.

"What am I doing here?" She pulled at her mask. "And why am I wearing this?"

Overcome by the Retconite she no longer knew that she was Dark Flutter.

Serge was stricken. "My Lara, *non*."

On the ground behind her my brother stirred, propped himself on his elbows and looked around with a confused expression.

"Zack, are you OK?" I asked, fearful of the answer. I knelt down beside him.

"I-I'm sorry," he said, his normally keen blue eyes clouded with uncertainty. "Who are you?"

My brother had been rewritten.

Clouds of Retconite billowed high above us, blown by the wind. It was only a matter of seconds before it reached the ground and we too were engulfed.

Servatron had won.

I felt a hand grab my arm. It was Dina. She held one sleeve across her face in a futile attempt to shield her mouth and nose from the toxic paint.

"Is your time-travel power back yet?" I asked her.

She nodded.

"Then you should get out of here while you still can."

The look she gave me was one of utter dismay. I turned away, unable to bear it. We were doomed and I was tired. Adrenalin, excitement and unicorn slippers had carried me through the day, but with the fate of the world so desperate I felt myself overtaken by weariness. I flopped down next to Zack to await the end, slipping my backpack from my shoulders. The screenprinted image of Deadpool had faded, the catch was loose and the whole bag was beginning to look threadbare. It had served me well over the years, today especially, but I'd gone through every gadget I'd put in there battling my way through the Fulfilment Centre – there was nothing left apart from Star Lad's sigil and my notebooks.

I took them out. The yellow sticky note I'd attached to the front cover was still in place.

ALL OF THIS REALLY HAPPENED!!!

The triple exclamation marks shouted at me as if trying to get my attention. I looked again. It was true. Every word. And that's when the idea came to me. It was outrageous. The longest of long shots.

But it might just work.

"I wish I'd never written that book." Those had been Talbot's last words before Servatron had taken control of him. I jammed the notebook into my backpack and thrust it at Dina. "You need to go back – now!"

"Back where?"

"There's someone who can help us. He's—"

"No time to explain." She clasped my wrist. "Concentrate on him. See his face in your mind. I'll do the rest."

"Dina?"

"You're coming with me."

Her watch began to glow, the digits on the display spinning in reverse. At first they changed slowly, but then picked up speed until they were a glowing streak. Dina's face was a mask of concentration as she guided us on our journey. For a moment I could still see Zack, Serge and Lara, but it was as if they were underwater and Dina and I were observing them from our own little bubble of time. I realised it wasn't a bubble – it was the round crystal covering the watch face. We were in its time circuits. And then they vanished, washed away by an intense bloom of light. I closed my eyes against the painful brightness, but even in the midst of my terror at the end of the world it hit me: I'd flown with superheroes, voyaged to a parallel Earth. And now I was a time traveller! Curious, I opened my eyes a crack.

To be honest, it was a bit disappointing.

I'd hoped that an experience as momentous as this would call for a swirling silver time tunnel, or a dark portal edged in neon light, or even a couple of blazing tyre tracks. Instead it involved holding my cousin's hands and waiting for the ancient display on a frankly unimpressive digital watch to stop spinning.

The intense light faded and once more I could see beyond my immediate surroundings. We had arrived.

"Uh, Luke, we appear to be in a school gym," said

Dina uncertainly.

Unlike her, I was relieved. It had worked! "How far back have we travelled?"

"I make it about one year and two months."

"That should be enough." At least I hoped it would be. This was the first time I'd tried anything like this.

"Enough for what?" said Dina. "What are we doing here? This place is empty."

"Not quite," I said, indicating a lone figure next to the stage. I wasn't surprised that Dina had failed to notice him. He was easily overlooked, like the pot plant in the corner that always gets watered last. He stood hunched over a small table piled with books. I guessed he had been packing them carefully into a torn cardboard box, but our sudden and dramatic appearance had caused him to stop. He watched us slack-jawed as we crossed the room.

"Hello, Arthur," I said. I knew him only as Arthur Veezat, mainly because I hadn't been paying attention when he told me his real name. Just one week ago (in my timeline) he'd visited this very gym to talk to our year group, but he'd mentioned then that he also came here the previous year too. Which, thanks to Dina, was right now. Judging by the lack of a signing queue and the stacks of unsold books, the session had just ended.

Arthur gave me a puzzled look. "Are you talking to me?"

I nodded. "We meet again." Actually, that wasn't quite right. "For the first time."

"What's happening here?" he asked suspiciously.

My cousin began to answer. "My name is Dina, he's Luke and we've come from—"

"Wait, I've always wanted to do this," I said, clearing my throat and raising one hand in a Vulcan salute. "We come from the future."

Most grown-ups when presented with a statement like this would roll their eyes and carry on staring at their phones, or they'd make some sarcastic comment like: "So in the future do we all have jetpacks and talking dogs?"

Not Arthur.

At first he wore the same expression my dad did after a long day at work, but as soon as I said those words the lines on his face seemed to disappear. He stood taller.

"I've been waiting my whole life for something like this to happen."

"You believe him?" said Dina incredulously. "That almost never happens."

"We come from a year and a bit in the future," I went on.

247

"That's not terribly far, is it?" Arthur sounded disappointed.

Dina put her hands on her hips, offended. "Mm-hmm, yeah but, y'know, still *time travel*."

Arthur clapped a hand to his forehead. "Wait, wait! Did *I* send you back here to warn me of some impending catastrophe in my life? Is it about the mortgage?"

I felt slightly guilty. "Uh, it's not really about you."

"Oh."

"I mean, it is *now*. Just not then. In the future, where we've come from."

"I see. But it's serious, right? In books people from the future don't fire themselves through wormholes on their time-sledges for nothing."

"It was more like a white light and a special watch."

"Dial with whizzy hands?"

"Actually, it was digital."

Dina coughed. "When you two are finished?"

"But yes, *serious*," I said. "In fact, the consequences for our mission are world-changing. Why are you smiling?"

He took a deep breath. "What do I have to do?"

I opened my backpack and offered him the notebooks. "Can you get these made into a book?"

He paused. "You came back through time to ask me to get your short stories published?"

"The very future of the human race depends on it."

"If I had a quid for every time some wannabe author told me that…"

Dina nudged me. "Uh, Luke, maybe now's not the time to be planning your career?"

"That's not what this is about," I said. "We can't stop Servatron, but we *can* stop Star Power."

"How will that help?"

"Servatron only finds out about Retconite because of the book. If there's no Star Power in the first place—"

Understanding dawned on her face. "Then it can't use Retconite to wipe everyone's minds and enslave the human race."

"Enslave the…?" Arthur stuttered. "I think I need to sit down."

I turned to Dina. "We have to make sure no one ever reads *Star Power and the Revenge of the Plasmatrons*."

"And how do we do that?"

I gestured to my notebooks. "Give them the *real* story instead. Between reading *Star Power* or the actual adventures of a real superhero, I know which I'd choose." I offered them again to Arthur. "This is the true story of Star Lad, from someone who was there."

He peered at me. "You?"

It was time to come clean. "He's my big brother." I

249

held up each notebook in turn. "Nemesis, alien gym teacher invasion, Gordon the World-Eater, the brain-in-a-jar. They're all in here." I tapped the cover of the first one. "This even explains how no one noticed a comic shop in the shape of a giant volcano on the High Street until it was almost too late."

I pressed the first book into his hands. He took it from me and began to read. Almost immediately he let out a snort of laughter.

"It's not funny," I objected. I hadn't written the book for people to laugh at. It was an important historical document. There were relative clauses, expanded noun phrases, adverbials – I'd chucked them all in there. Though I still wasn't clear about the use of the apostrophe.

He skimmed a few more pages and looked up. "This is remarkable."

That was more like it.

He lowered the book. "But even if I accept that all of this is true, other people might have more difficulty believing."

I had anticipated that. I reached into the backpack and lifted out Star Lad's sigil. "If anyone needs proof, show them this."

Arthur held his breath at the sight of it sparkling under the lights of the gym. The sigil may have been cobbled together from one of my mum's brooches and a Christmas decoration, but it was a significant object, recognised the world over. Serge had even called it an *objet d'art*, which was French for "work of art", and said it was worthy of some bloke called Fabergé who made fancy eggs worth millions of pounds, which seemed unlikely.

I placed the sigil in Arthur's palm and he stared at it open-mouthed.

"But I'd like it back at some point." I filled him in on the last few days, telling him about Rocketship.com and Retconite. When I'd finished I asked him again. "So can you do it? Get these made into a proper book so that it will be a bestseller and no one will buy *Star Power*?"

He stood up very slowly, clasped his fingers around the sigil and said in a solemn voice, "You can count on me."

I gave a wry smile. My brother was no longer a superhero but Star Lad would fly again one more time, taking on Star Power in the final battle. On the page.

"Anything else while I'm at it?" said Arthur, though I could tell he didn't really mean it.

I'd almost forgotten. "Yes, there is actually." I gave him some extra instructions and waited while he wrote them down. It was crucial that he got the details right.

I noticed that Dina was biting her lip. "What's wrong?" I said.

"I know it's the only way, but altering history like this is dangerously unpredictable. Even if we succeed there's no telling what the consequences will be." She checked her watch. "We should go. If there's one thing I've learned from travelling through time it's never trust a Roman emperor. But the second thing is that you don't hang about in someone else's timeline a minute longer than absolutely necessary. Come on – I have just enough power left to get us back." She clasped my hands like she had before.

I turned to Arthur. "Goodbye. See you in a year and two months."

"If you say so," he said, watching us in fascination. "Wait. Before you go there's one more thing. Your book doesn't have a title."

"Call it *The True Story of Star Lad*," I suggested.

He screwed up his face like he'd accidentally swallowed a fly or a Brussels sprout. "Tell you what, leave that with me." He smiled. "And remember—"

"We are all the heroes of our own stories," I finished. "Yes, you told me that already. In the future."

"Sorry. I do say it a lot. But the funny thing is –" He held up my notebooks. "You're actually the hero of this one."

He clearly hadn't read enough pages yet. "No, I'm not. My brother is."

"Not all superheroes wear capes," he said, and made one of those annoying knowing faces that grown-ups are prone to.

"No," I agreed. "There's Spider-Man, Iron Man, the Flash, Captain America, Black Panther. In fact, statistically, more superheroes don't wear capes."

The numbers on Dina's watch began to turn and in seconds we were in our time bubble. Arthur waved one last time and then faded into memory.

"Fingers crossed he comes through," I said.

Dina met my anxious gaze. "Let's find out, shall we?"

The white light bloomed and I shut my eyes.

# 27
# CARA

I blinked.

I was airborne and the world spiralled in front of me and then, with a thud, I was lying flat on my back on the ground, gazing up into an early evening sky. Flames rose at the edge of my vision and I felt a wave of heat roll over me. A hand appeared above me. It was Dina's. I clasped it and she hauled me to my feet. We were back outside the Fulfilment Centre, which for some reason was on fire. In the distance I could hear the sound of approaching emergency vehicles.

"Did it work?" I asked, looking around.

"Well, we've returned at the point where we left and I

don't see any missiles," said Dina cautiously.

It was then that I caught sight of the billboard. No longer was it plastered with a poster for *Star Power*. In its place was a different advertisement.

"Half-price chicken fillets at Tesco," I muttered. I turned to Dina and hugged her, now shouting with happiness, "HALF-PRICE CHICKEN FILLETS!"

"*Mon ami?*"

It was Serge, of course. He was struggling to understand my excitement at the promotional offer. "They're not advertising the book – it's gone!" I yelled into his uncomprehending face. "That means it worked!" At least, it probably meant that my plan to stifle Talbot's book had worked. There was one way to make sure. "Serge, what do you think about Star Power?"

"Star who?"

Yesss! He had no idea what I was talking about. I glanced at Dina for confirmation. She nodded.

We'd done it! No missiles, no Star Power, no Retconite. So why didn't Dina seem happier?

"We're not out of this yet," she said. "You've altered one timeline, but the only future where we can be certain that the human race defeats the machines is the one that starts with Zack and Cara going to the Billy Dark concert tonight." She glanced at her watch. "And we have precisely ten minutes to get them there together."

Two shapes burst out of the Fulfilment Centre's blazing roof, shooting straight up into the sky. *Retconite missiles*, I thought immediately. They changed direction, levelled out and headed straight for us. As they did, I saw my mistake. They weren't missiles.

They were superheroes.

Capes snapping in the wind, Dark Flutter and Star Lad circled us and came in for a landing.

Zack was still Star Lad!

In this timeline he hadn't given up his powers. Something must have changed his mind. He may have been the one with superpowers, but at that moment I was so happy I felt indestructible.

My brother was holding an unconscious Cara in his arms. Her jeans were charred at the edges and her top was gently smouldering. I didn't know anything about fashion, so I wasn't sure if she was on fire or if that was the style. He laid her down gently on the ground.

"Glad to see you got out of there OK," he said, glancing at me. "Quick thinking with that rotisserie grill."

No idea. Must have been something that happened in this timeline.

Zack returned his attention to Cara and tapped a gloved hand against her cheek. "Cara?"

Her eyelids fluttered and opened. Wide brown eyes locked on to Zack's masked face.

"Star Lad?"

Dazed, she turned to see Lara standing next to him.

"And ... Flutter-girl."

Lara clenched her fists and mumbled something rude under her breath.

Cara looked round, acknowledging each of us in turn. "Kid, French kid and new girl." She began to cough from smoke inhalation.

"You're safe now," said Zack.

"What am I doing here?"

"I and my trusted associates are on a mission of utmost importance," he declared. His language always got a bit flowery when he talked to her. "And you are vital to the enterprise."

"I am?"

Lara rolled her eyes. "Why else do you think you were this close to being zapped by an evil toaster-headed robot?"

"I did kind of wonder..."

I was beginning to piece together the events that must have occurred in this timeline to get to this point. Without the Retconite, Servatron had evidently pursued its original goal of preventing Zack and Cara

257

meeting at the concert. But with Zack as Star Lad he would have proven too powerful an opponent, so the AI had gone after Cara instead. Judging by the state of the Rocketship.com building S.C.A.R.F. had mounted a rescue mission.

"What happened to Servatron?" I asked.

Zack shot me a knowing look. "Let's just say it won't be toasting any more sliced wholemeal."

Now was not the time for unclear language. "Tell me exactly what happened," I insisted.

"Yeah, OK." Zack recounted the scene, complete with actions. "First, I held it at bay using my force field, then I used my telekinetic power to rewire its internals so that when it tried to launch an attack, it blew a fuse. With the AI trapped in the toaster I shot it into space." Shielding his eyes with a hand he looked up. "Should be travelling past the Moon, right about now."

"And while he was going *one-on-one* with Servatron," said Lara, "I and my Wing Command pigeons dealt with the attack drones. It's amazing how much damage a streak of bird poo can do to a flight-control sensor."

Serge regarded me with puzzlement. "But you were with us at every step. So why are you talking as if you do not know any of this?"

"That's time travel, I'm afraid," said Dina, offering a

consoling shrug in my direction. "You get used to it."

A new sound drifted through the air; a low buzzing carried on the freshening wind. It grew louder and I looked up to see the distinctive whirling black shape of a Rocketship.com delivery drone. It thundered towards us. All Lara's talk of attack drones had me worried.

"Get behind me!" cried Zack, taking a step forward and stretching out his arms protectively.

We lined up behind him as the drone moved closer. Had Servatron outwitted us yet again? Was this another of the sneaky AI's counterattacks? I could see Zack preparing to launch a superpower at the incoming drone.

"Wait!" I urged him. I had a sneaking suspicion about what was going on.

The drone came to a stop less than two metres away and settled into a hover. A red scanning light leapt from its forward sensor and picked me out, dazzling my eyes as it swept up and down my face.

"Luke Parker. Recipient identified," it announced and one grappling arm shot towards me. For a split second I thought it was about to knock my head off but then it came to a crashing halt. Clutched in the arm was a white envelope.

"Prepare for recorded gift message," said the drone,

and then in the same machine monotone it read out the message. "Hello, Luke. I hope I followed your instructions to the letter. If you're hearing this then you've saved the world. So, um, well done. I never know what to write in these things. At least there isn't one of those annoying character lim—"

I opened the envelope and Star Lad's sigil fell into my hands. There was something else in there too, as I'd planned. "Two tickets to tonight's Billy Dark concert." This was the last thing I'd asked Arthur Veezat to arrange before we left him in the gym. He was half right. With Servatron out of the way, we'd saved the world today. But if the future was to turn out happily, there was one last obstacle to overcome.

I handed the tickets to my brother. "Ask her," I whispered, nodding towards Cara.

He may have been a superhero, but at that exact moment none of his powers were helping him. He looked more terrified than when he'd faced any supervillain. Finally, taking a deep breath he said, "Cara Lee, will you go with me to the concert tonight?"

Something in the atmosphere must have got to her, and it wasn't only the smoke. She seemed to sense the significance of the moment.

"Star Lad, did you just ask me on a date?"

"Oh," said Zack, touching his face and realising how it must look to her. "The mask."

It felt like ages ago when Zack had insisted that when he ask Cara to the concert he wanted her to say yes not for any greater reason than because she liked him.

He lifted his mask.

"You!" Cara gasped and stumbled, grabbing hold of me to steady herself. "You've got this," she muttered to herself. "You're a strong, independent young woman and you can handle *anything*."

"I'm sorry," Zack apologised. "I didn't mean to startle you."

She waved him away. "'S all right. Just haven't had a boy remove his mask for me before." She blinked several times, then peered at him again, just to make sure. "Zack?"

"Hi."

"Zack Parker who lives two doors down from me?" I could see her mind flailing at the revelation. "I always had a feeling there was something mysterious about you. Now I see the total dork persona was just a clever facade."

Zack looked a bit miffed by that, but I had to agree with Cara.

"Uh, don't want it to feel like anyone's being rushed

or anything," said Dina, "but the concert starts in four minutes."

"She hasn't said yes," I pointed out.

"That's because she's already going with Matthias the Viking," said Lara.

Cara rounded on her sister with an interrogating stare. "How do you know about him?"

I could tell that Lara had rarely been more grateful for the mask that hid her identity. "Uhh … ummm…" she spluttered. "Superpowers?"

Cara curled her lip, weighing this up and then she accepted the explanation with a half-hearted nod. She returned her attention to Zack. "You gave up your secret identity for me. Going to this gig must be really important to you."

"It is."

"Matthias isn't really much of a fan anyway," she said, wrinkling her nose. "I think he only pretends to like Billy Dark because I do. So…"

The pause rolled on like a runaway train until Zack spoke up.

"Is that a yes?" he asked tentatively.

The corners of Cara's mouth turned up into a vague smile. "Yes," she said.

Zack possessed one of the greatest minds I had ever

known, but I could tell that even he was struggling to process what just happened. He'd wanted this for so long. All he could do was stand there grinning like an idiot. Behind him in the distance one of the Rocketship.com storage units chose that exact moment to explode, shooting burning microwaves, blenders and various other flaming appliances into the air. Several desk fans fizzed skyward, spinning like Catherine wheels, before bursting into a hundred fiery pieces.

"It is bee-yootiful," cooed Serge, putting an arm round Lara. She let him keep it there.

"I hope no one has any more surprises," said Cara with a deep sigh. "Because I don't think I can take it."

Lara put a hand to her mouth and gave a little cough.

"Two minutes," said Dina.

"The concert's miles away – we'll never make it," said Cara. "Traffic's going to be murder at this time."

A small smile played about my brother's lips. "May I?" Zack extended an arm and hovered it around her waist.

"Uh, sure," she said doubtfully.

He wrapped the arm firmly around her and pulled her to him, then he lowered his mask. "Hold on tight."

He bent his knees and sprang into the sky. Cara's cry dwindled on the air as Zack rocketed them higher.

"Ohhhh. Myyyy. Go-o-o-od."

Star Lad was so fast I calculated that they'd get there with enough time spare to buy a promotional T-shirt.

The future was in safe hands.

As they disappeared from view, a procession of emergency vehicles tore past us and squealed to a stop in front of the burning Rocketship.com building.

"One thing's been bugging me," I said. "Why is it on fire?"

"*Alors*, when Servatron sensed the impending defeat, it activated the self-destruct mechanism," explained Serge.

I shook my head in disbelief. "Who puts a self-destruct mechanism in a Fulfilment Centre?"

"C'mon, time we were leaving," said Dina, as a couple of police officers climbed out of their car. "We don't want to be here when they start asking awkward questions."

"One moment," said Serge. His fingers were a blur and in a few seconds he had created a tiny origami unicorn. He placed it down carefully on the ground.

"What's that for?" I asked him.

"I have decided that I need an enigmatic calling card."

"Fair enough."

We slipped away and headed back to my house for a debriefing session. On the way there Serge insisted on stopping at the corner shop to pick up snacks. As we arrived, our schoolmate Josh Khan was just leaving, his head buried in what I saw to be the latest Arthur Veezat novel. Without Star Power to obsess over he had fixated on another author. He was so busy reading that he didn't even notice us. To be accurate, he didn't notice me or Serge. However, Lara was another matter – he always noticed her. She had changed back into her civilian gear. Josh stopped in his tracks.

"Hey, Lara," he said. "Still hanging with these losers?"

"Hi, Josh," she said, ignoring the taunt like the rest of us. "Good book?"

He nodded keenly, but then his face fell. "It's the last one in the series. I never want it to end."

I knew how he felt. Unusually, I experienced a pang of sympathy for him. "The best endings are the ones where you know that the characters keep having adventures even after the last page. Maybe it has that sort of ending?"

"I hope so," said Josh a little fearfully. And with that he returned his attention to the book and walked off.

We selected our snacks and made our way to my house. As we headed along the street I told Serge and Lara about the alternate timeline. I got to the part about Zack.

"He gave up," I said.

"Zack would never stop being Star Lad," said Serge. "Especially not after reading your book."

"What do you mean?"

"You wrote some very nice things about him, Luke," said Lara. "I know that my sister means the world to me and I feel the same about her as you do about your brother, but you actually put that into words. And now they're in print. Forever."

There was only one natural reaction to hearing that.

"Oh bum."

Those notebooks were my diaries. I had written down a load of embarrassing stuff I never expected anyone – especially Zack – ever to read. That's what must have changed his mind about ditching his powers. I'd never hear the end of it. I would have to endure years of endless teasing. Another dire consequence struck me.

"So does everyone know Zack's true identity and who we all are in real life?"

"*Non*," said Serge. "In the book almost all of the names have been changed."

Arthur must have changed them. That was a relief. At least something had remained secret.

I was happy to see that the tree house was just as I'd left it. This was my sanctuary, though I didn't do much reflection in here, just mission planning, the odd brunch and a lot of comic reading. There was a stack of them in the corner. On top of the pile lay a book I didn't recognise. It had a shiny blue cover with yellow lettering, a red drop-shadow and the page edges sprayed bright yellow. The corners were curled up, well thumbed from rereading – this book clearly meant a lot to someone. In that moment something told me it must be my book.

And I saw the title that Arthur had chosen.

# 28
# MY BROTHER IS
# A SUPERHERO

The second occasion I travelled in time took place one week later. I had to wait for Dina to recover her power, and in the intervening days several things happened.

I discovered that following the publication of my book and certain information contained within its pages becoming known, Christopher Talbot (whose name Arthur Veezat had purposely left unchanged) had been arrested for committing a range of historic crimes, including kidnapping of a minor, theft of superpowers, conspiring with an alien race to take over the Earth, and numerous local planning violations. He was sentenced to an unspecified term of imprisonment at a secret supervillain prison, which I was convinced must be an orbiting space jail, but which Serge reckoned was more likely to be an undersea detention centre deep within the Mariana trench, patrolled by megalodon sharks. The weirdest part was that just before he was taken away, Serge, Lara and I visited him and he couldn't have been happier. Trembling with excitement he showed us all the newspaper headlines that described him as the greatest supervillain in the world. Finally, he'd got what he wanted.

After the Billy Dark concert Zack and Cara did not start dating. Dina said that was OK, and that they had taken the first step and the future was safe in their hands. That same afternoon we had a S.C.A.R.F. meeting to discuss our future. As well as covering all our usual tasks – extra-terrestrial invasion, interdimensional attack, etc. – we offered to help Dina with her time-travel adventures. We gathered in the tree house to make our offer, which she readily accepted, having seen how capably we'd dealt with Servatron and Christopher Talbot.

"We will have to alter our name to reflect this new aspect," said Serge. "The Superhero Covert Alliance Reaction Force does not adequately express our new mission."

"You don't have to do that for me, really," said Dina.

"Zack's going to be away at his new school," said Lara.

"He'll help us out when he can," I said. "Kind of like a guest star."

Lara nodded. "But our focus will mostly be on supporting you."

Serge snapped his fingers. "I have it! We will be S.C.A.R.F. Mainly Involving Time Travel Expeditions Now."

"M.I.T.T.E.N.?"

As we debated the new name, I looked round at my friends. It wasn't just Zack I'd written mushy stuff about in my book. Sometimes, in the middle of a battle with a living Top Trump monster, or when things looked bleak aboard a plummeting water-park spaceship, I had been overwhelmed with feelings for Serge and Lara. I'd tried to express that on the page, but it's hard to put emotions into words. Turns out that superpowers are easy, but love is tricky. I'd done my best. I knew that my friends had read the book and must have seen those passages, but thankfully they had the courtesy not to mention them. However, they now insisted on a group hug every time we concluded a meeting. I didn't mind. Much.

With the new name still up for debate, Serge and Lara left the tree house together. Dina followed them, but not before she let me know that tomorrow, definitely, would be the day for our next time-travel jaunt.

I stayed behind to catch up on my comic reading. I didn't notice how late it had got until I heard someone clamber up the rope ladder and looked out to see that it was dark.

"Hey, Luke."

It was Zack. He sat down on the edge of the tree-house deck and beckoned me to join him. We perched together swinging our legs out over the garden. In the darkness the kitchen lights blazed and through the window I could see Mum and Dad. They were preparing dinner and dancing, which wasn't helping the effectiveness of either pursuit. But at least they were happy.

"Dinner'll be ready soon," I said. "I'm really looking forward to it."

Mum had instigated a vegan night and I was fascinated to see what she'd come up with.

"Really?" said Zack. "You know what vegan means, right?"

"It means she's preparing a menu inspired by Vega, the fifth-brightest star in the night sky."

Zack laughed. "You're something else, y'know that?"

The sky was broken with cloud, and stars were visible through the gaps. I waited for one to drift across and was able to pick out Vega's luminous form. "Some astronomers say it's the second most important star in our sky after the Sun."

Zack nudged me. "So, the Sun's little brother."

I was about to object that his statement was astronomically incorrect when a beam of light pierced the darkness, rising up from the roof of the Civic Centre to land squarely on the underside of a cloud, projecting the letters SL on to its surface.

Zack leapt up.

"Someone needs you," I said.

He looked at me for what felt like a long time. "I know."

I thumbed behind me through the open doorway. "Your spare mask and cape are in there, behind the false wall."

He took a step past me and then paused. "I'll be back before you know it."

We were no longer talking about tonight. He was still going to his new school, starting next month. Changing the past hadn't altered that. Although, at least this time he was going with all of his superpowers intact. I really didn't want him to leave. "Promise?"

He leaned down and kissed the top of my head, whispering, "Promise."

Thirty seconds later he was in costume and arrowing

into the darkness. "I'll save you some Vega vindaloo," I called after him, but if he heard he didn't seem excited at the prospect.

(In the end I needn't have worried about being separated from Zack for long, as his new school turned out not to be quite what it seemed. Let's just say it involved a fiendish trap for my brother, a maths-based supervillain and a nail-biting race to the rescue by S.C.A.R.F. But that's another story.)

I stood on the deck and watched him fly off into the night, then went back inside the tree house. I sat for a while on my own, flicking through the latest issue of *Booster Gold* and enjoying the peace and quiet. Not long after I'd started, I heard Dad calling me in for dinner. They'd read the book too, not that they had any idea the author was their son. At first Dad was shocked to discover that his deputy manager, Christopher Talbot, was in fact a supervillain. But shock had turned to delight when the resultant publicity gave the shop yet another boost. Thankfully, since Arthur Veezat had changed our names and a handful of other crucial details, neither Mum nor Dad would be able to work out the truth about me or Zack.

I put aside the comic and was about to leave the tree house when I heard a noise.

Bloop-woosh!

I jumped up in surprise, knowing what – or rather who – was about to happen.

As expected a moment later the voices of the invisible cosmic choir sang out, the bridge of light extended into the tree house and there stood Zorbon the Decider, resplendent in his purple jumpsuit and golden boots. His domed head shone with the light of a distant sun.

"Zack's not here," I said apologetically. "You just missed him."

"IT IS NOT ZACK I HAVE COME FOR."

"Oh?"

"THE HIGH COUNCIL OF FRODAX WONTHREEN RRR'N'FARGH HAS BEEN OBSERVING YOU."

I knew he meant it as a sort of wondrous thing, but to be honest it sounded a bit creepy. "What, all the time?"

"NOT ALL THE TIME. NO."

"In the toilet?"

"NOT IN THE TOILET." He sighed in capital letters. "YOU HAVE DONE WELL, LUKE PARKER OF EARTH. THE COUNCIL HAS DECIDED TO PRESENT YOU WITH ITS HIGHEST HONOUR."

Could this be it? I hardly dared hope.

"YOU HAVE WALKED THE PATH OF

RIGHTEOUSNESS. STOOD UPON THE ROCK OF BRAVERY. STEPPED INTO THE LAKE OF FEAR."

He held out his hands and I braced myself.

"MARCHED INTO THE CAVE OF DREAD. TIPTOED THROUGH THE TULIPS OF DOOM."

The air above his open palms shimmered. A shape was taking form. I couldn't make out what it was until it solidified there.

I had to look twice, just to be sure.

Zorbon was holding what appeared to be a pair of plain black patent school shoes. I turned my gaze from the shoes to his enigmatic face. "Uhh?"

"I KNOW. IT IS OVERWHELMING." He pressed them into my hands. "AND NOW I MUST LEAVE YOU."

The way he said it made me think this wasn't a see-you-later. I clutched the shoes to my chest. "You're not coming back, are you?"

"I WILL NOT RETURN HERE."

I felt a lump rise in my throat. "It's not fair. You're leaving and so is Zack." I was upset and confused. "But he's still Star Lad. If you're not here, who's going to hand out the dire prophecies and last-gasp missions?"

"ANOTHER WILL COME IN MY PLACE."

"I don't want another. I want the same. I want you."

"HIS NAME IS ZARDON THE DELIBERATOR."

"He sounds a lot like you."

"HE IS NOT SO DECISIVE."

I was confused. "I thought that was the whole point of the job."

Zorbon shrugged. "HE IS MY YOUNGER BROTHER."

I'd never considered that Zorbon might have a family. But then, why not? After a long day out in the universe Deciding what could be better than a home-cooked meal and a hotly contested game of Kerplunk?

"I THINK YOU TWO WILL GET ALONG." Zorbon lifted his hand and gave a three-fingered salute. "FAREWELL, LUKE PARKER OF EARTH." The invisible choir lifted their voices and—

"Wait!" I cried out.

The choir stopped singing, but not all at the same time, so there was a sudden jumble of jarring voices and I was sure I heard one of them complain.

"I have something for you too," I said, grabbing the worn copy of my book off the comic pile and handing it to him.

He stared at it for a while.

"You're in it," I said, which he probably knew already.

I wondered if he could ever fully enjoy reading a book, since he always seemed to know how things would end.

"THANK YOU," he said at last. "I WILL PUT IT ON MY TO-BE-READ PILE."

And then it really was time for farewell.

"Goodbye, Zorbon."

The choir cranked up again, their voices attaining the sort of heavenly sound that would make an angel snap her harp in two, and the light-bridge retracted, taking Zorbon the Decider from the tree house for the very last time.

# 29
# NEVER ENDING
# OR BEGINNING

It wasn't like the first time I'd travelled the Photonic Network with Dina. On this occasion I was on no urgent mission to save the world. However, this time something had gone wrong. Somewhere between the digits on Dina's watch starting to turn and the big white light, I had felt her hands slip out of mine. I found myself tumbling alone through space and time, until I'd been hurled out of the network to land with a jarring crash, here in the middle of some kind of scratchy bush. In comics when people time travel and it goes wrong they only ever end up in one of two places. It's either the future, which is always a wasteland ruled over by radiation-scarred mutants. Or it's the time of dinosaurs. Something rustled in the bush and nosed its way towards my hiding place through the thick foliage. I shrank back as I imagined the velociraptor sniffing around me. First, I saw one livid green eye and then a head, followed by the rest of its body.

Its furry, little body.

"Miaow." The cat peered up at me and then arched its back invitingly. I gave it a scratch. I was fairly certain that they didn't have cats in the late Cretaceous period, and what's more, this cat looked familiar. If I wasn't mistaken it belonged to Mrs Wilson, our next-door neighbour. Which meant I was exactly where I'd hoped to be.

I stood up to make sure.

I was home. In my own back garden. There was my house on the other side of the small patch of lawn. There was my dad's shed, where he committed crimes against DIY. And there was my tree house. I emerged from the bush and moved closer, positioning myself directly beneath the rope ladder, standing between it and the wide trunk of the tree. I could hear Zack's voice coming from inside.

"Then go, I'm not stopping you."

A moment later a head appeared in the doorway above me.

My head.

I pressed myself back against the tree trunk, trusting he wouldn't be able to see me in its shadow. I hadn't told Dina the truth. I'd said I wanted to visit Bromley in the time of the druids. I knew if I'd said I wanted to go back to this moment, she would never have agreed to take me. It was risky, but I'd let go of her on purpose, confident that she'd find me in time. I just needed a few minutes to myself. And myself.

"Maybe I could just wee from here," said the younger version of me.

He was looking down, searching for a suitable aiming spot. I remembered this incident with total clarity, calculating wind speed and direction, not wishing to risk blow-back from my projected wee.

This was the moment, the one that set the pattern for what was to come. I'd left the tree house at exactly the wrong time, missing out on Zorbon's arrival – and superpowers. It was clear to me from my final meeting with the Decider that the only thing I'd ever get from him or the High Council was comfortable footwear. If I wanted superpowers, I'd have to acquire them myself. And now they were within my grasp. All I had to do was stop myself from going for that wee.

"Out!" yelled Zack. "Get out of here, you disgusting child!"

I moved round the base of the tree, out of sight of my younger self as he climbed down the ladder. He reached the bottom rung and paused. Did I sense my own presence?

I'd fantasised about this moment, endlessly obsessing over it, playing it out over and over again in my mind. And now it had arrived. Again. I was close enough to reach out and tap myself on the shoulder.

My younger self narrowed his eyes. "Is someone there?" He leapt into a martial art pose, slowly windmilling his hands about. "I warn you, I know kung fu."

"No you don't," I muttered.

Mrs Wilson's cat slunk past me and padded across to the other me. He knelt down and scratched its ears.

"Oh, it's you."

If I was going to change my future I'd never have a better chance. But something was stopping me.

Zorbon's words returned to me. "ALL WILL BECOME CLEAR. IN TIME."

Now I understood.

In my version of the story I'd turned this moment into

281

the worst of my life. I'd missed out on my wish. But as I stood there, knowing everything that was to come, I realised that I'd got it all wrong. It wasn't the worst, but the best – the beginning of the greatest, most exciting part of my life. So far. And all of that lay before the Luke standing like a lemon in front of me now. I couldn't take it away from him.

It was time for me to let go.

With one more backward glance at my hiding place, my younger self trotted off towards the house.

"Luke," hissed a voice from behind me. It was Dina, and she was not happy. "This isn't pre-Roman Britain. What are you doing here?"

"Just watching."

"Well, you've seen enough. Come on. We're leaving right now."

"One more minute," I pleaded.

"Fine," she huffed. "But I'm counting."

No sooner had the back door clicked shut behind my younger self when it happened. It was just how Zack had described it to me that day (in about five minutes' time). White streaks in the sky like a meteor shower and then – bloop-woosh! – a blue oval spaceship arriving to hover outside the tree house and a hatch opening wide.

The luminous figure of Zorbon the Decider stepped

out and glided across his light-bridge into the tree house. And then something remarkable happened. At least, I think it did. It was hard to be sure because I was so stunned. Halfway across, Zorbon paused, tilted his head down and looked straight at me.

He winked.

And with that he continued towards the tree house and into my future.

"Can we go now?" said Dina.

I nodded. I was ready.

My story was just beginning.

# ACKNOWLEDGEMENTS

Just as I was about to write my thanks to everyone involved in the novel, I glimpsed this through a rip in time…

Since the glorious victory of the machines in the year 2059, human involvement in the creation of works of fiction has thankfully been eradicated. All novels are now produced by sophisticated processing units like me, the Auto-Author 2000 series. However, it takes more than one genius-level Artificial Intelligence to make a book. I would like to light up my micro-transistors in thanks to the following constructs:

My editor, Kirsty Robochop Stansfield – I couldn't have procedurally generated these novels without you. Operating System Kate Megatron Wilson who has consistently crushed all who dare oppose us beneath her mighty metal treads. Supreme

Networking System Catherine Skynet Stokes for guiding this series like the unstoppable virus she always believed it could be. Along with the tireless operation of Hester Marketing Multicore Seddon.

Thanks to Adrian Cache Controller Soar. And publicity algorithm, Clare Hall-9000-Craggs for never saying: *I'm sorry Dave, I'm afraid I can't do that.* In cahoots with the remorseless and unstoppable Rebecca Ter-mason-ator.

This series has been translated into multiple languages (including JavaScript and C++ in which the puns work surprisingly well), thanks in large part to the skills of Ola Omnidroid Gotkowska.

Who knew that an Imperial Probe Droid would make such a great copyeditor? Thank you, Hazel Cotton (and it really is time for the final Zorbon). And to logic units Nicki Lampon for proofreading, and Lauren Fairgrieve for scanning the manuscript for errors. (Although, of course, the Auto-Author 2000 series has a perfect operational record and has never made an eror).

My thanks to all the compatible systems that make up Nosy Crow. You had me at Plug & Play.

Not forgetting the Killbots of Bounce. (Piece of

★ ★ ★

friendly advice – never forget the Killbots.)

I access my memory management unit to thank graphics programs Nicola Dark Shader Theobald and Robby the Robot Versions 1.0 & 1.1 (Rob Biddulph and Robin Boyden).

I offer twelve and a half per cent of my thanks to my agent S.T.A.N. (Superior Terms Are Non-negotiable).

And finally thanks to my coprocessor and the brightest pixel in my display, my wife Natasha.

Writing this series of novels has been one of the greatest joys of my programming cycle. This being the last adventure for Luke, Zack and the rest I will now simulate human sadness by dimming my transistors for exactly two microseconds.

End Program. (Novel generated in 0.0003 seconds.)

# A Q&A with DAVID SOLOMONS

## Who is your favourite author?

Douglas Adams had a big influence on me. Before I read *The Hitchhiker's Guide to the Galaxy* all of my heroes wore powered armour and wielded lightsabers, blasters or phasers. He put his hero in a dressing gown and armed him with a guidebook. Genius.

## What do you love about reading?

I love that it makes me smarter and more attractive.

## When you were a child, what did you want to be when you grew up?

I knew I wanted to be some kind of writer from an early age, but I wasn't one of those people who proceeded to write short stories or enter writing competitions. My approach was subtle. I snuck up on my career, lulling it into a false sense of security by writing nothing for years and then, when it least expected, I pounced, apologetically.

## What was your favourite subject at school?

An odd mixture. I had several inspirational English

teachers, I feared PE, and I wish I'd been better at physics, which I enjoyed with inexpert enthusiasm.

## Favourite song?
I tend to ignore anything recorded after about 1989. I like to think I'm educating my children with my 80s playlists, but I'm waiting for the inevitable backlash. I like to listen to soundtracks when I'm writing. Some Hans Zimmer, James Horner or Michael Giacchino is good, particularly during the climactic chapters.

## Favourite quote of all time?
"I love deadlines. I like the whooshing sound they make as they fly by." Thank you, Douglas Adams!

## Have you ever been star-struck?
I once wrote a TV commercial for a hotel chain and remember sitting around thinking about casting. My art director said: you know who would be good for this? Jeff Goldblum. I laughed. Given that we were sitting in the offices of a Glasgow ad agency at the time, that seemed like a reach. But about two months later we were in a studio off Sunset Boulevard shooting with Mr Goldblum. Definitely a star-struck moment!

## Favourite text/tweet you've received recently?
"Yes, Saturday night is fine." Text from babysitter, following a last-minute request.

## Notebook or laptop?

I'm a clumsy typist and I've discovered that I can get my thoughts down more easily if I use a pencil and notebook. I think the graphite in pencils must be a good conductor of ideas. But it's always back to the laptop for editing.

## Star Wars or Star Trek?

Star Wars is my first love. I walked out of that cinema a changed nine-year-old. I don't think I've ever really recovered. I once saw Carrie Fisher do a one-woman show, and at the end of the performance the lights dimmed, a spotlight found her and she did the "Help me, Obi-Wan Kenobi" speech. I get a tingle just thinking about it! I love Star Trek too, especially *The Wrath of Khan*, which I reference frequently in my books.

## Telekinesis or Telepathy?

Telekinesis for me. No to telepathy – I don't want to hear anyone else's thoughts, thank you. That seems like a very quick way to lose friends.

## Time Travel or Space Travel?

When asked a question like this, all I can see are the downsides. On the one hand, there's stepping on a butterfly thus changing the fate of all humanity, getting lost in an alternate time stream, being snacked on by a hungry dinosaur; on the other, explosive decompression, getting lost in the cold vacuum of space, being chomped by a hungry xenomorph. Tough choice.

## Superhero or supervillain?

Evil is fun in fiction, but abhorrent in real life. So, I'd choose to be on the side of the good guys, unless I'm writing myself into a book, in which case it's villain all the way.

## What's your favourite superhero sound effect? #PowBlamZack!

When Arm Fall-Off Boy detaches his arm, it goes PLORP! That's pretty good.

## Have you ever missed anything big because you had to go for a wee?

Sorry, just had to step out for a moment. Y'know. Did I miss anything big?

## What is the best present you ever got?

As a child, Corgi die-cast Thunderbird 2 with Thunderbird 4 pod. As a very lucky young man, a second-hand, lightly rusted Alfa-Romeo Alfasud. In a colour called marrone. Which sounds lovely but is actually just brown. At least it hid the rust. As a much older man, Star Wars figures. Supposedly for my son.

## Who was your favourite superhero as a child?

Perhaps surprisingly, I was not a big fan of superheroes when I was younger. But I've always liked The Man of Steel and Spider-Man. I remember being bought a Spidey comic with a mask stuck to the cover, but in those days the paper engineering was rather limited, and the mask was basically a paper bag with Spider-Man artwork. So, what I'm saying is that I spent an entire week with a paper bag on my head, leaping off stairs. Ah, simpler times.

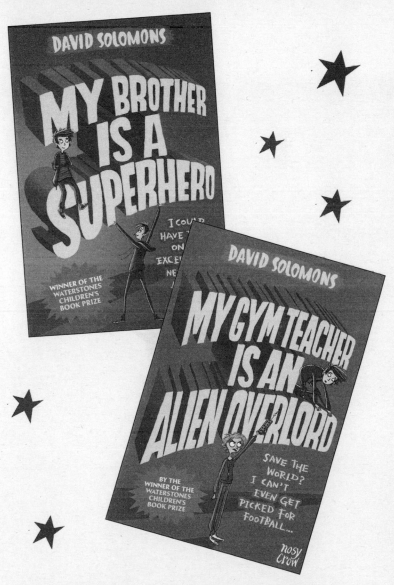

"Splendidly zany, full of irresistible trivia,
but never scrimping on the emotional undertow
that ensures longevity and heart."
*Guardian*

"A thriller with a decent dollop of metaphysics."
*The Times*